When Magic Shows Up at The Door

G. Wedel

When Magic Shows Up at the Door
Copyright © 2024 by G. Wedel.
All rights reserved.
Published by G. Wedel
ISBN 979-8-883-64290-5
First Paperback Edition: March 2024
Printed in the United States of America

No part of this book may be used or reproduced in any manner whatsoever without permission, except in the case of brief quotations embodied in critical articles and reviews.

Contents

Chapter 1 - The Elves' Art Fair 1

Chapter 2 – Galton's Sword 41

Chapter 3 - Paul's Wedding 63

Chapter 4 - The Frog from Hell 95

Chapter 5 - The Green Diamonds 129

Chapter 6 - The Moorish Princess...................... 159

Chapter 7 - The Crystal Water Lily.................... 177

1

The Elves' Art Fair

Paul was eating fried eggs and toast, while his sister Rebecca, standing in front of the sink, was washing the dishes.

"Will you come home for lunch today?" she inquired.

"No, I'm going to the Art Fair," he answered dryly.

"In Green Wood?" she asked with apprehension, moving away from the sink and sitting at the breakfast table, across from her brother.

"Yes, of course. That's where the Art Fair usually takes place," he replied with a wide, warm smile. Rebecca was not easily appeased.

"It's dangerous," she said, lowering her voice to a whisper.

"You know that I go to the Art Fair every year. The elves are my friends!" said Paul, who in reality had no friends at all, and strongly believed that friendship was an anti-economic practice. He poured a strong cup of tea for his sister and refilled his own cup.

"But Paul…they are magic!"

"Yes, they are and they are also happy to see me, because every year I buy a large quantity of products at their fair," he said, ending the conversation and getting up from the table.

"Be careful…anything can happen in the woods!"

Paul left, feeling slightly annoyed. *Women always worry too much*. He sighed with relief at the thought of not having a wife. He actually looked forward to the Art Fair, where he purchased paintings, furniture, and decorative objects made by the elves, which he resold, tripling the price he paid. He was a very shrewd merchant and not afraid of meeting the elves in Green Wood. Business was everything in Paul Callahan's life. Day after day, week after week, month after month, he worked constantly to grow his clientele and increase his reputation of junkshop dealer in the county. In reality, his shop was no longer a junkshop. Over the years, it had turned into a store that could supply any type of house furnishing, antique or modern, that his customers desired.

Paul lived with his sister Rebecca, who dutifully cooked his meals and took care of his house. She had settled in her role of housekeeper, while he provided the financial security that she couldn't have had on her own. He considered their life together as one of his business accomplishments. When Rebecca had fallen in love with David Rosen, the town baker, who had been courting her insistently, he had quickly ended their romance before its inception. One morning, he had paid a visit to David Rosen in his bakery. After ordering a dozen pastries, he had addressed a sly speech about how a baker's financial status was unsuitable for his sister. David Rosen had retreated into desperate solitude. Not comprehending David's sudden coldness, Rebecca had withdrawn into sad resignation. Satisfied with his victory, Paul had continued to apply himself happily to his business deals, certain that after each workday he would find a speckless home and a delicious home-cooked meal.

Paul decided to make a brief stop in his shop before heading to the fair. Cedric, his apprentice, was meticulously checking a tea set, recently acquired at a flea market, in one of the neighboring towns.

"Anything new?" Paul asked.

"Yes, the silver vase on the counter," Cedric replied, without taking his eyes off the teapot he was inspecting for possible cracks or chips. Paul glanced at the tall silver vase, which contained a pink rose.

"Did you put this flower in it?" he asked, perplexed.

"Of course not. That's how it came."

"Came from where?"

"I don't know. I found it in front of the door, with a note attached that said: *"With gratitude, Haralda."*

Paul smiled, pleased with himself.

"Who is Haralda?" Cedric asked, staring at a teacup, afraid of probing too deeply into Paul's personal life.

"She's a witch. A couple of years ago, I helped her find an 18th century chandelier for her dining room. She never paid me with money, but she told me that she would reciprocate the favor. I'm not sure about the value of this vase as compared to that of the chandelier, but it's good to have friends in the right places!" he added with a dark undertone. Cedric agreed gravely.

Paul picked up the heavy vase to inspect it. It had a round base, an elongated shape, and a handle decorated with silver leaves. As he touched the rose, a loud scream followed by a series of sobs echoed inside, startling him. He bent his head towards the opening of the vase and yelled, "Who's there?" The voice continued to sob desperately, without answering. Paul grasped the flower and shook it up and down. The small head of a beautiful young woman instantly rose from the opening of the vase.

"Leave the flower in there! Don't touch it!" she screamed. Both Paul and Cedric faced her in astonishment. She had the angry expression of a bad-tempered child.

"Who are you?" asked Paul.

"I'm Princess Ilena of Breckenridge-Northrop, betrothed to Prince Richard of Somerville-Langford, which means that one day I'll be Queen Ilena Breckenridge-Northrop-Somerville-Langford!" she enunciated with haughtiness.

The two men bowed their heads respectfully.

"What are you doing in there?" Cedric asked.

"I'm trapped! Can't you see? I'm trapped with this precious rose, which I have to keep alive with my tears," she replied, starting to cry again. The tears flowed profusely into the vase, and the rose emanated an intense fragrance.

"Why is this rose so precious?" Cedric asked.

"The life of this rose is linked to the life of Prince Richard, the man I love, my future husband!" she answered, shaking the rose angrily.

"Who trapped you in there?" Paul inquired.

"Haralda, that horrible witch! She shrunk my body and told me that I have to stay in here until one of her spells takes effect. She didn't tell me what her plan was. She never even told me how long I have to stay here! This is so disrespectful, especially considering that I belong to a royal family. Don't you agree?" the princess said, banging her little fists and kicking her feet inside the vase.

"Yes, Your Highness" the two men acknowledged, at the same time feeling a pang of fear in their chest, as they heard the name of Haralda the witch.

"I'm so sorry!" Paul sympathized with Princess Ilena, while he kept a guarded distance from her predicament.

"Sorry? Is that all you have to say?" Princess Ilena reacted with indignation.

"I'm deeply grieved and I understand that you're in a terrible situation," he continued. Princess Ilena grabbed the rose stem, protruded her arm out of the neck of the vase, and struck Paul's face repeatedly with the flower.

"Sorry isn't good enough! What are you going to do about it? Are you just going to stand there and say you are sorry?" Her eyes burned with fury.

"Easy! You'll destroy the rose!" said Paul, blinking to remove a flower petal stuck on his eyelashes. "There is not much we can do," he continued, while Cedric nodded in agreement.

"I'm sure there is! Pusillanimous men! You must help me or when I get out of here, you'll be very, very sorry!" She stared at them with the determination of a spoiled brat.

"All right!" Paul said, always ready to find an accommodation. "I'll talk to Haralda. Does that satisfy you?"

"Yes, and be quick because I'm tired of sitting inside this vase," she said, sliding down and resuming her sobs, while the rose immediately seemed to acquire an intense coloration and a very soft texture.

"Leave the vase on the counter! I'm going into the woods. I'll stop at Haralda's place after the Art Fair," Paul told his apprentice.

"Sure," Cedric acknowledged with the undertone of someone who had grown callous to the supernatural.

Paul left the shop feeling a little dispirited. He drove his largest pickup truck into Green Wood and reached the area where the fair was held. A large number of visitors walked through the trees, across a large field, stopping at the artists' stands to check the merchandise and make their purchases. Paul parked his truck and worked his way through the crowd. From a distance, he saw Rodney's stand and decided to examine his furniture, which was always highly in demand. Rodney used different types of wood to inlay or laminate his furniture. He preferred modern, light-colored, curved shapes, but to satisfy all tastes, he also made traditional oak or walnut pieces, polished and sometimes lacquered. Rodney was an important supplier for him.

While he was crossing the grass clearing to reach Rodney's stand, a large abstract painting, exhibited on an easel, attracted his attention. A small crowd was gathered in front of it. Horace, the security elf, and Heloise, the green fairy, could not recognize any shape on the canvas. They whispered to each other their dislike for modern art. Bartley stood proudly next to the artwork, which had been painted by his friend Marjorie. He answered questions and pointed out the title, *Trees in Springtime*. As he was an eccentric and intellectual type of elf, Bartley wore a pair of distressed jeans and a tea shirt, printed with a striped Piet Mondrian design. Next to Bartley, Marjorie smiled and blushed, amazed by the enormous number of elves, fairies, and sorcerers present at the fair. The previous day, she had been kidnapped by Renalda the witch and saved by Bartley, cementing a solid friendship with this elf. Attending the Elves' Art Fair and being introduced to the magic community that resided in Green Wood was an extraordinary experience, accessible to very few humans like Marjorie. Captain Jack Sanders, another human attending the Fair, held his wife Lodema the witch by her waist, making appreciative remarks about the shades of the leaves, which, apparently, he had no problem recognizing on the canvas. Lodema smiled radiantly at her husband, happy to be with him at the fair. She enjoyed drifting from stand to stand, engaging in conversation and exchanging news. The Art Fair was a very important social event in Green Wood.

"Hello, Paul," a cheerful voice saluted Paul Callahan from behind. He turned and smiled warmly.

"It's wonderful to see you, Haralda!" he said.

"How did you like the vase?" she asked him, with a shadow of mischief in her gaze.

"Of excellent taste. Is it particularly valuable?"

"You're the expert, Paul, but don't underestimate that vase: it has exceptional powers, although they're not obvious," Haralda replied. Her eyes sparkled like a starry sky.

"What kind of powers?"

"You'll know when the time is right," she said, starting to take her leave.

"Wait!" he stopped her. "What about the woman inside? She says she's a prisoner."

"She is, indeed! She's part of a spell and, unfortunately, she'll have to wait for a certain turn of events before she can be released."

"Isn't there anything that can be done to…"

"No!" Haralda interrupted him. "Besides, when did you turn soft-hearted?"

"I'm not soft-hearted! She's a princess and… very irritating…"

"I know, I know," Haralda said soothingly. "I assure you that things will change…for everyone. You won't be the same man and life will seem different to you." Paul was confused by her words.

"What should I do with the vase?" he asked.

"Anything you like, Paul. It's yours. You can keep it, sell it, or give it away. No matter what you do with it, the spell won't change. Now I have to go," she said, rushing away and vanishing in an instant.

He shook his head uncomprehendingly. It seemed to him that his job had become very difficult lately. This business of the princess in the silver vase was quite upsetting. He decided he was going to sell the vase as soon as possible. The sudden beat of a lively marching band made him focus again on Marjorie's *Trees in Springtime*. For a few seconds, his imagination floated among the senseless, green brushstrokes on the canvas. A group of Norwegian elves led the parade, playing the drums. They were followed by a group of Scottish elves that played the bagpipes, and by a delegation of German elves playing the accordions. The onlookers whistled and applauded. It all seemed very surreal to Paul, who had no interest in music.

He dismissed the show as nonsense, and decided to purchase Marjorie's painting. To the amazement of Horace and Heloise, he paid a large sum of money for *Trees in Springtime* and walked away, feeling very satisfied. He knew that he could resell the painting to Dr. Dillingham, his dentist.

Trees in Springtime would have looked very sharp in the dentist's waiting room, above the magazine table. Holding the large canvas, he walked in the direction of Rodney's stand. Suddenly, he heard the sound of an explosion. A cloud of sparks enveloped the painting, giving him a stinging sensation on his hand and arm. After the luminous cloud had dissipated, he realized that the painting had shrunk to half its original size.

"Rylan, the goblin!" a young elf woman, wearing a flowery lilac dress, exclaimed with a strained voice.

"What sort of witchcraft struck my painting? I want my money back," Paul mumbled, staring at the shrunken *Trees in Springtime*.

"I wouldn't worry so much about the painting… Have you seen your clothes?" she said.

Paul looked at the sleeves of his shirt, which were creased into deep folds. Then he noticed that his pants also exhibited waves of fabric along his legs and, worst of all, he had the feeling that his belt was loose, no longer holding his pants tightly around his waist.

"What in the world! I shrank too!" he cried in horror.

"Definitely the unmistakable trademark of Rylan the goblin!" the tall elf Dalbert murmured. He was wearing a tall conical hat with swirls of burgundy, radiating clockwise from the top, and was holding the hand of his German fiancée, Wilfreda.

"A dangerous elf! Very dangerous!" Wilfreda said, pressing her massive body against Dalbert to seek protection. Paul stared at the moving diagonal stripes on Dalbert's purple hat and felt slightly dizzy. He didn't like magic.

"What are you going to do?" Wilfreda asked him.

"First of all, I'm going to get my money back!" Paul said, regaining his business composure.

"That won't help you regain your size. You'll have to confront Rylan the goblin," Dalbert told him.

"Who is Rylan the goblin?" Paul asked in exasperation.

"He's a short elf sorcerer who likes to shrink his victims, when he casts his spells."

"How short is a short elf? Is he a real elf, whereas you are gnomes?" he asked.

"We're all about five feet tall with some exceptions," Dalbert explained. For example, Wilfreda and I are taller, but we are all elves."

Paul took in this disquisition on the size of elves distractedly, while tightening the belt around his hips.

"What does Rylan look like?" he asked.

"He's about three feet tall. He has red hair and a bushy red beard. He always wears an orange hat and…well…you'll see him if you find him," Dalbert replied.

"Can you help me find him?"

"No, I keep away from him. I don't want to be shrunk."

"I can help you!" the elf with the lilac dress offered.

"Esther! Are you crazy?" Wilfreda cried, pulling her sister a few feet away to have a private conversation. "Why would you want to help this human? He's selfish, greedy, and insensitive; he exploits his apprentice paying him a meager salary, and he disrespects his own sister. He's a very sad human, who has no friends and no interests in life, except for making money. Why would you want to risk your life for him?"

"I don't know…he looks like a child who needs help and possibly, beneath his harsh disposition, he may have some feelings. Maybe he'll learn something from this experience…"

"Experience? You call knocking at Rylan's door an experience? He's a crazy elf! He spends his time dancing with witches in the woods," Wilfreda insisted.

"I sort of like Paul…he's clever and very successful in his business…he's hard-working and…he has beautiful black eyes," Esther confessed in a whisper.

"Seriously! You actually like this man! I hope you're right. I hope there are unrevealed facets to his personality beyond his appearance."

Esther threw her head back, while her long blond curls bounced in all directions. Her eyes sparkled in anticipation of the adventures ahead. She was a bold elf, who liked excitement, and was not afraid of taking risks. She hugged her sister with affection and then joined Paul.

"My name is Esther and I'll take you to Rylan's house," she formally introduced herself. Esther stood in front of him, ready for action. He recognized his own drive and determination in her. He liked her. However, Paul was careful and mistrusting of all women. He had built a mental shield to protect himself from any kind of emotional attachment because he liked the way he had organized his life. He didn't need any complications.

"Perhaps it would be better if a man could undertake this task that, as I understand, is not going to be easy and safe," Paul suggested.

"No one will want to take this task. It's in your advantage to accept my offer because I have dealt with Rylan once before," said Esther.

"What do you expect in return?"

"I don't expect anything. I accomplish what I set out to do and you don't have to be concerned at all." She charmed him with her positive green gaze, into which he unwillingly became absorbed for a few seconds. She perceived his vulnerability and, most of all, read an immense loneliness in his eyes. Paul liked the fact that she didn't seem to worry excessively as women always did. He allowed himself to follow her lead, not having an alternative.

"Let's go and quickly complete this mission. I'm a man with many responsibilities: the entire county depends on my business."

"Just a minute," Rodney, the elf-artist, stopped him. He wanted to help Paul whom he regarded as a patron of the arts. "Take this magic charcoal pencil. Whatever you sketch will become real." Paul took the pencil with a grateful smile. In reality he was very dissatisfied. He didn't like magic. He didn't like being the protagonist of this ridiculous story. As he was about to leave, his heart was filled with foreboding.

"Good luck!" said Wilfreda.

Like two epic heroes marching toward the battlefield, Paul and Esther left the fairgrounds, while everyone stared in silence. The news of Paul's shrinkage had quickly spread throughout the wood, leaving its inhabitants in a state of apprehension. As soon as Esther disappeared behind the trees, Wilfreda began to cry desperately. Dalbert hugged her, while the stripes on his conical hat turned a bright shade of red. The marching band resumed its lively tune, but a feeling of impending doom hung over the fair.

"Rylan lives in a small castle on the branch of a sycamore tree," Esther broke the silence. "Any human or elf approaching his castle, within a radius of two miles, turns smaller." Paul dropped the painting he was holding in his hand. It hit a rock and its frame cracked, producing an unpleasant sound that reverberated among the trees. He stopped to pick up the pieces.

"I already shrank. Will I turn even smaller?" he asked.

"The size of a wildflower."

"What does Rylan want from me?" Paul asked.

"Elves know more information than humans do. We're not really supposed to share this information, but in this case, I think you deserve to know what's happening, particularly in light of the fact that you're risking your life," she said with a thoughtful expression.

He looked at her and felt safer. She seemed in control of the situation. He looked at the folds that wrinkled her face and at her dainty pointed ears, which had become familiar to him, and smiled. She really made him feel comfortable. She saw his smile and for the second time, she perceived a boyish vulnerability in him.

"Rylan has been trying to take over the Kingdom of Somerville-Langford for years. He has succeeded in shrinking the rightful King James to a size that has made him invisible to the human eye," she began her account. "His wife, Queen Dora, talks to specks of dust, convinced that one of them is her husband.

"That's probably true," Paul advanced.

"Except that no one knows where the king-speck of dust is, and probably he's not in his castle. I'm sure that Rylan holds him captive to prevent Haralda the witch from reversing his spell."

"Is Haralda the witch involved in this story?"

"Oh yes, Haralda and Rylan the goblin are arch-enemies."

"In my shop, I have Princess Ilena of Breckenridge-Northrop, trapped by Haralda in a vase. She's trapped with a rose and cries to keep the rose alive with her tears. She says that the life of the rose is linked to that of her fiancée, Prince Richard of Somerville-Langford," said Paul.

"Isn't love wonderful?" Esther smiled romantically.

"It's actually quite pathetic," he corrected her, with no feeling for romance. "What happened to Prince Richard?"

"He also disappeared. Rylan had begun to shrink him, but Haralda devised the counter-spell of Princess Ilena to keep him from disappearing like his father. As long as she cries and keeps the rose healthy, he won't shrink anymore. He is still visible, but small," Esther explained.

"How small is he now?" Paul asked, at the same time noticing an apple on the ground, which seemed to be the size of a basketball. He looked upwards and realized that the trees had grown taller and that probably he would have had to use both hands, besides a ladder, to pick an apple.

"When Haralda cast her spell, Prince Richard was about three inches tall. He disappeared from the castle and his mother fears that a stray cat may have preyed on him," Esther continued.

"Horrible!" said Paul, unsure if his words were referring to Prince Richard or himself. They walked a short distance silently, while their steps made a delicate sound on the gravel.

"What does Rylan want from me?" Paul asked for the second time.

"He wants the vase with Princess Ilena."

"He can have it! I can't even sell it with the annoying princess crying inside of it," said Paul.

"Giving the vase to Rylan does not guarantee that he will reverse your spell. Do you want to keep shrinking until you disappear?"

Paul looked at the painted canvas he was holding, which was now the size of a large stamp. He shook his head in dismay. The only positive development was the fact that his clothes had been shrinking as well. Therefore, his sleeves and pants were fitting him properly now. A loud, deep buzz startled them. They turned their heads and saw two enormous bees flying in their direction. Paul and Esther started running and a wild chase ensued. Paul turned his head to check the distance of the two insects and crashed into a large mushroom. He pulled his face out of the cap and brushed pieces of gills off his shirt. Then he ducked, while the bees flew over him. The insects made a couple of loops.

They briefly flew downwards, and they spun in the opposite direction, again heading toward Esther and Paul. The two friends ran, unable to find a place to hide. Like synchronized jets, the bees coordinated their flight, making a few eight figures in the sky. Then, they followed a zigzagging pattern and a wide corkscrew. Finally, they aimed in the direction of the running couple, continuing their chase.

Paul and Esther saw a passing squirrel and quickly jumped on it, starting a wild ride. The squirrel climbed a tree and leaped from branch to branch, without a purpose. Esther screamed, desperately holding onto the squirrel's fur. Paul had his arms tightly wrapped around one of the squirrel's legs and his hands attached to the squirrel's tail. Both of them were dragged along the trunk of the tree, repeatedly hitting their head and their back against it. Finally, they loosened their grip, falling downwards, and landing on a thorny blackberry bush. The bees charged them. Paul detached himself from the thorns of the bush, somersaulted on a patch of moss, and balanced himself on his legs. Then, he searched his right pocket and extracted the charcoal pencil that Rodney had given to him. He quickly sketched a net, on a rock. The net became real. As soon as the bees were at close range, he trapped them, ending their fine display of air acrobatics. Esther jumped off the bush into Paul's arms. He gently deposited her on the moss and ran to get some dew with a leaf. He helped her rinse the cuts she had on her face, arms, and legs. Using both hands, he also picked a few blueberries from another bush to quench their thirst with the juice. He saw the canvas of *Trees in Springtime* intact on the ground. He was pleased because he was still planning to have Rylan reverse its size, in order to be able to sell it to Dr. Dillingham.

Slowly, the two friends resumed their walk through a meadow, feeling protected by the long stems of the flowers, which reached Paul's chest and the top of Esther's head. A small country mouse, panting frantically, ran in their direction and collided with Paul. He fell to the ground, trapping the mouse's tail under his body. He slowly got up and brushed the dirt off his sleeves, while the mouse quickly ran off. Suddenly, a red and black cat leaped between him and Esther chasing the mouse. It was Gorman, Renalda the witch's cat. Esther lost her balance. Paul extended his arm to help her back on her feet, but he was not quick enough and Gorman, forgetting about the mouse, pounced on the elf, seized her with his teeth, and ran off. Esther screamed, kicking her legs. Horrified, Paul began to chase Gorman, but the cat was much bigger and faster than him and vanished through the flowers. He sat on a rock and remained motionless for some time. He couldn't decide what to do. He considered the possibility of interrupting his mission and returning home, but he knew he would have been unable to resume his normal life in his miniaturized state. Gradually, a new feeling quite unknown to him, began to take hold of his heart. It was a feeling of immense loneliness, which was intensified by the dark shadows that the evening was casting over the wood. He missed Esther's companionship, her bouncing curls, her facial grooves, and her vibrant personality. The silence of the night was now broken only by the occasional cry of a crow. A cold breeze made him shiver. He wrapped himself with some large leaves and sat on a rock, leaning against the trunk of a tree. He was unable to sleep. His eyes were suddenly filled with tears that streamed down his cheeks. They were warm, heavy tears that trickled on the ground, producing a sharp crackling sound.

"Why are you crying?" a bright, silvery voice asked him. He turned his head and saw the tiny figure of a young woman, sitting on the low branch of a tree. She was blond and blue-eyed. She was wearing a long, pink gown, and was gently flapping her small wings.

"Who are you?" he asked.

"I'm Chloe, the tree fairy. Tell me why you're so sad."

"I'm afraid that my friend Esther may be dead," he answered.

"No, she's not dead. She can take very good care of herself," Chloe reassured him, "and you, Paul, I see that you're not dead either: your heart is not as cold and hardened as one would have thought!"

"Where's Esther?" he asked.

"You'll meet her in front of Rylan's castle. I'll help you because the lives of others depend on you. Normally, I take the shape of a nightingale, but since we have to rush, this time I'll transform myself into a faster bird," she said. She twirled, resembling a small pink tornado. Gradually, the tornado widened, emitting sparks, and blowing the leaves on the ground in all directions. Paul gaped in disbelief. The moonlight shone through the trees. It spread its bright light over the spinning tornado. Paul intensely disliked magic, but was getting used to its frequent occurrence, although it conflicted with his solid sense of logic. The contour of an eagle became clearly visible, as the bright light of the small vortex dimmed and died into the night.

"Get on board and hold onto my feathers!" Chloe said with a raspy voice.

Paul was surprised to see that she still had blue eyes. He sat between her shoulders and grasped her long, soft feathers. She flapped her powerful wings a few times and took off.

Gorman had carried Esther through the woods, enjoying the cruel sensation of control he had over her. A diabolical spark of evil flashed in his yellow eyes. As Esther screamed loudly, Gorman tightened his teeth on her, with even greater satisfaction. Suddenly, she pulled his whiskers and elbowed his nose. The cat produced a long, guttural meow, opening his mouth. She rolled to the ground and quickly found refuge underground, sliding through an opening that she found among the roots of a large tree.

As his pain subsided, Gorman proceeded to insert his paw into the opening, trying to reach Esther with his claws. She lay flat on the ground, holding her breath. After a few failed attempts, Gorman gave up and left.

Esther carefully emerged from her shelter and walked toward Rylan's castle. She was standing in front of the sycamore tree, on which Rylan's castle was built, when Chloe arrived. The eagle glided toward the ground, with fully extended wings, and gracefully landed among the trees. Still exhilarated by his fantastic ride through the night sky, Paul stepped onto the ground in a daze. Chloe quickly transformed herself into a nightingale, her favorite animal form.

"Good luck!" she said and flew away, singing.

"I was so worried about you," Esther said.

She reminded him of Rebecca, but this time he wasn't annoyed.

"I'm glad you are all right," he said, "I thought I had lost you forever."

"Never say forever! Humans have a very warped sense of time: it's always too short or too long. Always remembering the past or waiting for the future! I like to live in the present and I find the concept of time quite deceitful."

She was very sensible, he thought. He had been very lucky to be matched with such an extraordinary elf. The hoot of an owl from the top of the sycamore tree diverted their attention to the castle. It was black, made of stone, with barred openings on its walls. It had an asymmetrical shape and eight turrets of different height, connected by bridges. The dark outline of the castle against the sky inspired dismal feelings.

"Did you say you have been here before?" he asked her.

"Yes…" she answered hesitantly, trying to hide her face behind her bouncing curls.

"What happened?"

"It's not a very nice story. You have to promise me you'll never mention it to anyone. My sister Wilfreda and her fiancée would be very upset."

"I promise."

"Last year, Rylan shrank Dalbert in order to take one of his magic objects: Galton's Sword, a sword that makes anyone who uses it invincible."

"Who's Galton?" Paul interrupted her.

"A blacksmith who lived 200 years ago. He had magic powers because his mother was a witch."

"Did Rylan get the sword?"

"I had to give it to him! He told Wilfreda that unless he had the sword, he wouldn't let Dalbert regain his original size, and Wilfreda was so upset she couldn't bring the sword herself."

"You allowed Rylan to become invincible with the sword? Why didn't you take away his power using the sword?" asked Paul.

"It's not that simple. Wilfreda was losing her mind over Dalbert's spell. I thought that eventually, later, we could figure out a way to get the sword back. Luckily, Rylan never realized how powerful the sword really is," she explained.

"You did the right thing!" said Paul, who had questionable values when it came to attaining his goals, during the performance of his business activity. "We think alike!" he added.

Esther ignored Paul's appreciative comment and, facing the castle, she recited loudly:

"Coleridge, Coleridge
Let down the drawbridge
Lead us fast to your master
We'll reverse the disaster."

Immediately, Coleridge, who was Rylan's elf guard, released the drawbridge, which produced a deafening squeak. He also released a rope ladder, allowing them to reach the tree branch on which the entrance of the castle was located.

"Good evening, Lady Esther," the elf guard greeted her with deference. "Is this man a friend of yours?"

"Yes, he's looking for Rylan."

"My master is not here tonight. He's in the woods. Would you like to rest for a while and have some refreshments?" Coleridge asked.

"We wouldn't mind having something to eat and drink. We had a very difficult day," said Esther.

"Please come in," he said, looking more like a butler than a guard.

"What beautiful paintings and furniture!" Paul commented as he was walking through a hallway leading into a large living room. Coleridge cleared his throat and, totally ignoring him, resumed his conversation with Esther.

"By any chance, did you remember…ahem…the small favor I asked…" he said, lowering his voice.

"Of course, I did!" Esther replied. She rummaged in one of her pockets and extracted a tiny book, the size of a small coin, handing it to him.

"Haralda the witch shrank the book so that I could carry it here. You can reverse the spell by placing it under the light of a full moon, at midnight," she explained.

"How lucky! We have a full moon tonight!" he said with childish enthusiasm. "Life in the castle is so slow and dreary. There's not much for me to do here, besides raising and lowering the drawbridge." He looked at the book with a spark of happiness in his sad eyes.

"It's about magic adventures, set in an Irish wood. You'll like it: it's filled with human emotions," she said.

"I certainly need some of those in this castle!" Coleridge said.

"Where exactly is Rylan?" Esther asked.

"Clover Green, on the south side. That's where he meets the witches. If you really have to go there, take this," he said, giving her a lizard skin. "It spoils the effect of anything prepared in the cauldron."

Esther thanked Coleridge, who left the room to get some refreshments.

"Paul! Where are you?" she called.

Paul's voice echoed through the castle, "Third room to the right!"

She found him standing in front of a large painting that depicted a rural dance, in an Irish village.

"Seventeenth- and eighteenth-century paintings on every wall! The antique furniture is authentic!" he said excitedly. "Maybe I could convince Rylan to sell some of his paintings and furniture. I could charge so much money in my shop!" he added, temporarily forgetting his shrinkage problem.

"You could, but remember that Rylan is not interested in money. He likes specific objects that he can use," she said.

"I could ask for some of the paintings and furniture when I exchange the silver vase with the annoying princess."

"I'm sure you could. However, you should first help Princess Ilena," she said.

"I suppose…" Paul muttered without conviction, while climbing the leg of a chair. He stood on the chair to admire a painting, from a higher level.

"Why should I get involved in the distressful business of the Kingdom of Somerville-Langford and of the annoying princess?" he asked.

"We already are involved in this business and we have to help Princess Ilena and Prince Richard because they're in love and deserve to be reunited," Esther lectured him.

Paul did not cherish romance and chivalry. He thought that saving the princess required a great amount of time and energy that he could channel into something more lucrative. However, he was also well aware of the fact that he needed to regain his original size.

Coleridge entered the room, carrying a tray filled with two thimbles full of Port and a platter of cookies, broken into small pieces. Coleridge picked up the two shrunken friends and gently placed them on the table, where they ate and drank.

"We have to go now," Esther announced.

Coleridge escorted them to the entrance, and released the squeaking drawbridge and the rope ladder. He waved goodbye, closed the drawbridge, and retreated into his private tower. There he held under the moonlight the book that Esther had given to him, while the clock slowly struck twelve times. The book grew in size and Coleridge sat comfortably on an armchair, in front of the fireplace, ready for hours of entertainment in the cold, solitary castle.

Paul and Esther reached Clover Green slightly after midnight. They witnessed an unexpected pandemonium. Six witches sang and danced wildly, around Rylan the goblin.

Each witch had long hair of a different color: black, blond, brown, white, purple, and red. The witches' robes matched the color of their hair. Their skin radiated a bright light that was blinding to sustain. Rylan's orange cap barely contained his red curls, which were as long as his beard. Numerous earrings pierced the large lobes of his pointed ears: a moon, a star, a hatchet, a black cat, a broom, a pumpkin, a skull, an eye, a key, a ghost, and other Halloween symbols. His eyes were the shade of copper. He looked diabolical. He kept his hands on his hips and kicked his feet up and down, at the beat of the witches' song. The moonlight was spread out over them, emphasizing the incongruity of their bizarre presence in the darkness of the night.

Esther and Paul watched the hellish scene, hiding behind the thick foliage of a low bush. The witches broke their circle. Almira, the white-haired witch, and the youngest one in the group, engaged in a polka with Rylan, following the music that magically came out of a hollow tree trunk. An owl, with glassy eyes, stared at them without moving. Paul wondered if the owl was alive or made of stone. He thought that if it had been a little statue, it could have been sold as an interesting, decorative object.

Hilda, the blond witch, and her red-haired sister, Tilly, walked through the black smoke, produced by a hot cauldron. They added wood logs to the fire. Fiona, the brown-haired witch, and Marlena, the black-haired one, began to add magic ingredients into the cauldron. Each addition inflated the viscous green mass, bubbling inside the cauldron, to the point of eruption. However, each time, the swollen green mass imploded with a loud 'swoosh' and collapsed into a viscous substance, while a foamy condensation leaked out of the gigantic black pot. Edrea, the purple-haired witch, and the oldest one in the group, held a prism in front of the cauldron, focusing her blue gaze on it. The prism spread a dark blue light that enveloped the cauldron. The polka music ceased. Rylan and Almira stopped dancing. The owl remained motionless.

Rylan and the witches stood in a semi-circle around the cauldron. A few dark clouds partly covered the full moon. Esther shivered slightly and Paul held her hand tightly. Rylan took his cap off and extracted a tiny human figure.

"Hail to Prince Richard!" shouted the witches, dancing in a state of frenzy. Rylan held the shrunken prince with one hand, over the cauldron. Almira laughed and yelled, "Shrink him! Turn him into a speck of dust!"

"Drown him!" said Hilda.

"Crack him like a twig!" Tilly suggested.

"Melt him in the bubbles!" Fiona screamed.

"Dip him into the cauldron!" cried Marlena.

"The Kingdom of Somerville-Langford will be yours! You shall be our king!" Edrea said triumphantly.

"The Kingdom of Somerville-Langford will be mine, all mine!" Rylan repeated, while the curls of his long hair and beard moved sinuously, like snakes.

"He's an evil elf! Please Paul, save Prince Richard!" Esther pleaded, shaking a little. Paul didn't wish to anger Rylan and his mad witches to save Prince Richard, whom he considered already doomed.

"There's nothing I can do! We're dead if they see us," he said.

She suddenly remembered the lizard skin that Coleridge had given to her and took it out of her pocket.

"Coleridge said that it neutralizes the cauldron spell. I'm going to save Prince Richard," Esther said, taking a few steps forward.

"Are you crazy? Rylan will throw you into the cauldron and turn you into a speck of dust!" Paul stopped her.

"You don't seem to care!" said Esther. "We don't think alike!"

"Yes, we do!" he said, angered by Esther's stubbornness, which was a reflection of his own mulish personality.

"I'll do it! You stay here!" he said, grabbing the lizard skin. He walked to the cauldron and swiftly dropped the lizard skin into it. He remained unnoticed by Rylan and the witches, who were wildly dancing and singing. Suddenly, Rylan loosened his grip and let Prince Richard fall into the cauldron, while the witches bellowed a loud scream. The fire died out and the content of the cauldron turned into lukewarm bath water. Prince Richard resurfaced and held onto the floating lizard skin. The six witches ran into the woods and disappeared. A cold breeze shook Rylan's long curls. Uncomprehendingly, he stared at the inactive cauldron.

"Rylan!" Esther called him.

"Did you undo the spell?" Rylan asked.

"Yes. I stopped the spell because I'd like to propose a deal," she replied.

"Let's hear your deal," he said, with curiosity.

"Just a moment, we are proposing the deal together," said Paul, stepping next to Esther.

"What a surprise!" Rylan remarked.

"I ask that you allow Paul, Prince Richard, King James, and me to regain a normal size," she said.

"…and that you turn this painting back to its normal size as well," Paul continued, holding the tiny canvas of *Trees in Springtime.*

"What do I gain?" Rylan asked.

"The Kingdom of Somerville-Langford," said Esther.

"I already have the kingdom without doing any of the things that you ask," said Rylan.

"We'll convince Haralda to let you keep the kingdom," Esther said.

"We'll be your allies," Paul added.

"Haralda is a problem, a very big problem... It's a deal, but if you break it, you'll regret it!" Rylan agreed.

Rylan pulled Prince Richard out of the cauldron and placed him next to Paul, who was holding Marjorie's painting. Then, he took a small pillbox out of his cap and opened it. With two fingers he extracted the invisible King James and handed him to the prince. Prince Richard put his father into his pocket for fear of losing him. Rylan closed his eyes and pronounced a magic formula. His orange hat levitated slightly above his head, and his beard rolled itself into a long cylinder. Finally, the beard unrolled, and the cap fell back onto his head.

"As you walk away from my castle, you will regain your natural size," Rylan said. Then he addressed Prince Richard, "You and your family must leave the Kingdom of Somerville-Langford." Finally, looking at Paul and Esther, he said, "I want the magic silver vase."

"I have one more deal to propose," Esther said boldly.

"Another deal?"

"Yes. I'd like to swap Haralda's silver vase for Galton's Sword," she proposed.

"…and some of your paintings and furniture," Paul added.

"No! Not the vase!" screamed Prince Richard. "First, you give away my kingdom and now…"

"We're trying to help you, Prince Richard. Everything will be fine for you and everyone else!" Esther interrupted him, without mentioning Princess Ilena's name.

"I really didn't have much use for the sword. What kind of magic powers does the vase have?" Rylan asked, apparently unable to use the sword and unaware of its real power.

"Haralda didn't tell me, but the vase is supposed to be a gift of value. She only said I would find out in time," Paul replied.

"I accept the deal," Rylan said, because he was a curious and foolish elf.

"We'll bring the vase tomorrow," said Paul.

"Tomorrow you can fill your truck with some of my paintings and furniture," Rylan instructed him.

Rylan returned to his castle, while Esther, Prince Richard, and King James walked in the direction of the village. Gradually, as Rylan promised, they regained their natural size.

"Why did you give away my kingdom?" King James asked unhappily.

"We had to do it. It was the only way to save your life and your son's life," Paul replied.

"Eventually, we'll figure out a way to regain the kingdom in the future," said Esther.

"How can you give away the vase with Ilena stuck inside?" Prince Richard objected.

"I'm sure that she's no longer in the vase. Haralda's spell was supposed to end as soon as you regained your normal size," Esther reassured him.

"When are we going to take possession of our kingdom?" King James and Prince Richard asked.

"Be patient!" Esther replied.

The following morning, as he opened the door of his house, Paul found Rebecca crying desperately, next to Cedric and his wife Gwendolyn. Rebecca screamed when she saw her brother.

"What happened in Green Wood? I was so worried when you didn't come home!" Then she noticed Esther and recognized her elf features, screaming a second time. "She's one of them! Did they kidnap you?" Rebecca asked.

"What happened in Green Wood?" Cedric inquired.

"It's a long story, but first let me introduce you to King James and Prince Richard of Somerville-Langford and to my friend Esther," said Paul.

"Friend?" Rebecca repeated, totally disregarding the royal guests. Paul proceeded to recount the entire story, starting from his visit at the Art Fair.

"Are you really going back to Rylan's castle tomorrow?" Rebecca asked.

"He seems totally infatuated with the elf," Cedric spoke softly into his wife's ear.

"Where's Ilena? Prince Richard interjected, interrupting the family reunion.

"Where's the silver vase?" Paul asked Cedric.

"I left it on the counter inside the shop," Cedric replied. The group decided to go to the shop and check what had happened to Princess Ilena. Paul carried *Trees in Springtime*, which had grown back to its original size, and gave Cedric instructions to sell it to Dr. Dillingham. They found the princess asleep on the floor, next to the counter.

"Ilena, Ilena!" Prince Richard gently shook her. She stirred and sat up, confused.

"What happened?" Cedric asked her, as he picked up the silver vase on the floor.

"I don't remember anything. I fell asleep inside the vase, with tears up to my waste, and now I'm here on the floor." she said.

"Haralda's spell has been reversed. You're free!" Paul told her.

"I knew you could do it!" she said, shaking Paul's hand with gratitude.

"However, there's a problem: Paul gave my kingdom to the evil sorcerer Rylan the goblin," said Prince Richard.

"How could you?" Princess Ilena addressed Paul with anger.

"I'm sorry. I had no choice."

"You're sorry? No! You can't tell me you're sorry and leave the problem unsolved! Take action immediately! It's an order!"

"Yes, Your Highness, I'll do what I can."

"That's not good enough! You'll do what needs to be done and deliver results as soon as possible or you'll be very sorry!" Paul bowed his head, very annoyed by Princess Ilena's bossy attitude.

"Paul, take the vase and let's go to my sister's house. She must be worried," said Esther.

"Are you going to the house of the elf's family?" Rebecca asked her brother.

"It's also our family," Paul replied, leaving everyone dumbfounded.

"We have business to take care of tomorrow," said Paul. He picked up the vase, wrapped his arm around Esther's shoulders, and left with her.

Paul retrieved his pickup truck in the wood and drove with Esther to Dalbert's mushroom-shaped house. Dalbert and Wilfreda were in the living room, surrounded by a small crowd of elves and other members of the magic community, including Bartley and his girlfriend Marjorie, Denby, Rodney, Horace the security elf, who enjoyed emergencies, and even Lodema the witch and her husband Captain Sanders. Esther knocked on the door and Wilfreda opened it. The two heroes were received with cheers, clapping, and whistles. Esther and Paul had to recount the entire story a second time. Dalbert was very happy to hear that Galton's Sword was going to be returned to him soon.

"How did you lose Galton's Sword?" asked Rodney.

"It's a long story!" Esther said, changing the subject. "The main thing is that everyone regained his normal size, and that Prince Richard and Princess Ilena were reunited." The elves cheered a second time singing together.

Wilfreda pulled Esther aside to talk to her privately.

"How are things going? Is Paul a selfish, callous merchant, without a soul?" she asked.

"He's kind, gentle, generous, brave, very astute in attaining his goals, and he has beautiful black eyes. Paul has a soft heart like all humans," Esther replied.

"I hope you're right," Wilfreda said, hugging her.

"We have to go back to Rylan's castle," Esther announced.

"Good luck with your next adventure in the woods!" said the elves. The couple waved goodbye and left.

2

Galton's Sword

The following morning, Paul and Esther drove through the woods, singing cheerfully together. A thick smell of moss permeated the inside of their vehicle, which bounced up and down, crossing over rocks and large tree roots. Unpredictability, excitement, and challenge filled their hearts.

The figure of an old woman, lying face down in the center of the road, interrupted their merriment. Her unkempt, white hair covered most of her shoulders and part of her hips. It concealed the woman's identity.

"Is she dead?" Esther asked, while Paul's pickup truck slowed down to a complete stop.

"Let's find out," he said, getting out of the vehicle. However, he was only able to take a couple of steps when the woman, suddenly, sprang up from the ground, and pointed her finger in his direction, uttering, "Stop right there, Paul Callahan! You thought you could deceive Rylan!" The young face of Almira the witch was flushed with anger and contempt. Her long, white hair had a silvery reflection under the sun. Her lips widened into a cruel, tremulous smile, revealing her large teeth. Esther also stepped out of the vehicle, but she was reluctant to move forward. The witch terrorized her. As an elf, she had magic powers, but they were no match for the strength of a witch.

"You and your elf friend are crooks! I won't let you get away with your ambitious plan!" the witch continued.

"We made a deal with Rylan," said Paul.

"There's no deal! I'll stop you and your friend from trying to cheat Rylan!" Almira said with a hoarse voice. She curved the long fingers of her right hand and pointed them at Esther. Then she widened them, discharging a set of red sparks and a silver flash that zoomed into Esther's direction and surrounded her entire figure. Instantly, Esther shrank in size and disappeared.

"Where is she?" Paul cried.

"In your silver vase. Now you can trade the vase for the Sword of Kester!" Almira's voice filled the wood with a loud, high-pitched laughter. Her black eyes burned with cruel joy. Gradually, her figure lost consistency and vanished, leaving the dying echo of her laughter behind. Paul opened his truck and picked up the vase.

"Esther! Esther, are you in there?" he called, feeling a knot in his throat. Esther slowly rose out of the vase, up to her waist. Her face had a bewildered expression.

"Are you alright?" he asked with a desperate tone.

"I'm fine...I think...just a little confused," she answered, as if she were awakening from a dream. He tried to pull her out of the vase, but in vain. No matter how much he pulled and how much she pushed with her feet against the inner surface of the vase, she could not come out beyond her waist.

"I guess I'm stuck in here," she finally conceded.

"What can we do to reverse the spell?" asked Paul.

"Let's go to Haralda's house. She'll know what to do," said Esther.

Paul placed the vase in the front seat of his truck, on his right side, and drove off in the direction of Haralda's cottage. Esther, protruding from the vase, looked out of the window silently, while tears rolled down her groovy cheeks. Paul felt the knot in his throat growing bigger.

"Don't worry, I'm sure we'll get through this," he said. He was not sure at all, but as an experienced salesman, he was able to inject conviction in his voice. Esther looked at him with sad, hopeful eyes.

He smiled, making her feel reassured. They reached Haralda's cottage in the late afternoon. The entire house was covered by jasmine and wisteria. These two plants crept over the walls, the pipes, the roof, and the chimney, leaving open spaces only for the door and the windows. They also covered the fence, surrounding the property with colorful cascades of flowers. The cottage had such a cheerful and pleasant appearance that it didn't seem to belong to a witch. The intense fragrance of the flowers made Paul and Esther feel a little dizzy. They found Haralda sitting at a small table, in her front garden, flipping a card she had just picked out of a stack. Paul approached her, holding the vase in his hands.

"I guess you don't want to get rid of your vase anymore," Haralda said reproachfully. Paul didn't speak. "The Queen of Hearts!" Haralda said, placing the card on the table. Then, she looked at Esther, and smiled benevolently.

"You're a lucky elf! He cares for you, Esther," she said. Then, suddenly, rising from her chair, she yelled "What have you both done?" Haralda was angry and, as all angry witches, she clearly exhibited her emotions in a peculiar way. Her eyes shone with the violence of a turbulent ocean, and her voice had a dark quality that made the trees shiver.

"We wanted to help Princess Ilena and Prince Richard," Esther spoke.

"In fact, we succeeded in having her, Prince Richard, and King James regain a normal size," Paul added.

"You call this success?" Haralda's voice boomed through the trees. "You left King James and Prince Richard without their kingdom, which now belongs to Rylan the goblin; Princess Ilena can't marry Prince Richard because he has no kingdom; the entire royal family is banned from the castle; Rylan's witches are angry with you; and Esther has been shrunk and trapped inside the silver vase! You call this success?" Haralda repeated angrily. Paul and Esther humbly lowered their heads in silence.

"Please, help us," said Paul, with a tone of desperation.

Haralda sighed and sat at her table, pondering the case for a few minutes. Finally, she addressed the couple with urgency in her voice.

"You must go to Rylan's castle and trade the vase for Galton's Sword."

"The vase?" Paul interjected.

"Yes, the vase, with Esther in it. Then, Paul, you must go to the Kingdom of Somerville-Langford, which is currently ruled by the Grand Vizier Moustafa, an evil sorcerer, friend of Rylan. You must hurry because the royal family is in danger. Take Galton's Sword: you'll need it!" said Haralda.

"In the past, did you tell me that the silver vase has magic powers?" Paul asked.

"Yes, it does, but you'll find out in due time," she replied. Then she looked at Esther, whose blond curls had lost their bouncing quality.

"You're a brave elf and you have a determined man next to you. Don't be afraid: love conquers all," she said. A squirrel scurried through the garden, climbed on the table, and ran across pushing the stack of cards on the grass. Paul started to pick up the cards.

"Leave the cards and go! There's not one minute to be lost!" Haralda said.

Paul placed the vase again in the front seat of his truck and drove off, zooming through the trees. He scared a family of rabbits that hopped aside. He nearly collided with Gorman, Renalda's wandering cat, who produced a deep, guttural meow, jumping on the branch of a tree and fleeing at supersonic speed. The silver vase was shaking, as the vehicle rocketed through the wood. Paul held it with his right hand, keeping his left hand on the steering wheel, without slowing down. As he began to approach Rylan's castle within the range of two miles, he noticed that the trees were growing taller and that his truck was moving through the underbrush. They reached the castle at sunset. Its eight turrets looked ominous against the bright red sky, on the branch of the sycamore tree. The drawbridge was down and Coleridge, Rylan's old guard, was waiting for them at the entrance.

"Welcome back!" he whispered. "The Master is on Clover Green with his six witch friends. He's enraged because he believes you were trying to deceive him."

"We know," Paul replied, holding the silver vase in his hand. Coleridge saw Esther's head, protruding from the vase.

"Lady Esther! How terrible! I'm so sorry!" he voiced incoherently.

"Don't worry, Coleridge, I'll get out of this predicament."

Holding the vase, Paul walked to Clover Green, where he witnessed an unimaginable scene. Rylan the goblin and the six witches were sitting in a dining room magically located on the branches of an oak tree. The long table and chairs were placed on a wide strip of yellow satin, connecting one branch to another one. Everything seemed to be weightless on top of the fabric. Two lit chandeliers were suspended above them from a high tree branch. On the tables there were two tureens filled with steaming cream of vegetable soup and several trays displaying a large selection of foods such as: baked ham glazed with brown sugar and pineapple juice, pork loins stuffed with apples and bacon, roast ducks with grapes and chestnuts, game pies with currant jelly, sausage stuffed onions, scalloped oysters, muffins, and different types of breads. On another table, placed on top of a strip of lavender satin, extended between two lower tree branches, was a large variety of desserts: cream puffs and other pastries, banana trifle and cherry trifle, custard pies, fruit tarts, devil's food cakes covered with fudge, persimmon pudding, scones, and marzipan cookies, shaped like black cats and brooms.

Concealed by a large bush, Paul and Esther stood petrified, inhaling the delicious smell that filled Clover Green. The witches wore long gowns that matched their hair color: brown, yellow, black, white, purple, and red. Rylan wore a suit and tie. His long red curls and beard against the black color of his suit, and the copper reflection in his eyes contributed to the overall diabolical atmosphere. Under the oak tree, a bubbling cauldron hissed and growled. A pink smoke rose from the pot, spreading a pleasant odor of cotton candy through the wood.

"When is the potion going to be ready?" Almira asked.

"We still have to add ingredients and pronounce the magic formula," Edrea replied.

"It smells good," said Rylan.

"It will taste better than it smells," said Hilda.

Edrea got up from the table and descended to the ground, sliding on a wide ribbon of silk attached to the satin strip. The other five witches followed her, lining up behind her. Edrea stared into the cauldron, while her deep blue eyes shone like the eyes of a cat. The pink bubbling liquid acquired a bluish tint, and the smoke rising from the cauldron seemed to have the same shade of purple as Edrea's hair. The old witch spoke softly, but clearly.

"Sticky, bubbly, syrupy sweet
We shall drink to bring deceit
The lovely princess can't see the danger
Her handsome lover will be a stranger."

Rylan's deep laughter echoed in the background. Edrea opened a small black box and each witch took a pinch of its contents adding it into the pot.

"Calendula will strengthen our power," said Tilly, the red-haired witch.

"Pink acacia will yield a transformation," said her blond sister Hilda.

"Valerian will erase memory," Almira pronounced with an unusually low-pitched voice.

"Hyssop will make the potion as forceful as the breath of a dragon," the brown-haired Fiona said, pirouetting like a graceful ballerina.

"Borage will enhance the effect," said Marlena, the black-haired witch, whose eyes had the metallic reflection of hematite.

"And peppermint will enhance the taste!" Edrea concluded.

"Rylan, come down! It's time to toast!" said Almira.

Rylan joined the witches, sliding down the ribbon of silk. Edrea clenched her right hand into a fist and opened it quickly. Immediately, a cup appeared in the right hand of each one of them. Edrea took the ladle hanging from one of the handles of the cauldron and began to serve the purple potion.

"It really smells delicious! I'd love to taste it!" said Paul.

"We have to stop them!" Esther whispered.

"We're not going to interfere and cause any more trouble!"

"But we did so much to reunite Princess Ilena and Prince Richard. With this spell she won't recognize him! Please, do something!" Esther insisted.

Paul looked straight into Esther's eyes and said drily, "There's nothing we can do! We'll follow Haralda's plan without getting off track."

The witches and Rylan made a toast. They cheered, "Lovers will be strangers!" They drank the potion and started dancing around the oak tree.

"Oh no! The spell has been cast!" Esther said. "If you care for me, throw the entire contents of that black box into the cauldron. It should alter the spell," she instructed him.

"All right, I'll do it for you!" Paul yielded, shaking his head. As Haralda had pointed out, the "Queen of Hearts" had been played. He swiftly approached the cauldron, unseen, while the diabolical creatures sang and danced wildly in a circle. He picked up the black box and emptied it into the cauldron, quickly moving away. The effect was instantaneous. A puff of black smoke was ejected from the cauldron, while several splashes of potion hit the witches. Rylan, protected by the trunk of the oak tree, was the only one who remained dry. The witches turned into six small goats, each one of a different color and began to fight with each other. Horrified, Rylan tried to hold the white goat, Almira, who was his favorite witch. However, she kicked him, totally unaware of his identity, as well as that of the other witches, and resumed her fight with them.

"Almira! Almira!" Rylan cried with tears in his eyes. The witches attacked each other viciously, with their horns. Again, Rylan attempted to separate Almira from the herd, but she rammed him, making him roll against a tree. Then she charged him and rammed him two more times with her head. Finally, she joined the fighting goats that were running away, chasing each other. Rylan got up slowly. His forehead was bleeding and one of his shoulders was hurting. Paul came forward.

"I'm here to keep my part of the deal," he said, handing the silver vase with Esther protruding from the top.

Rylan stared at the vase, emotionless.

"Very good," he said, ignoring the pain and the blood trickling on his beard. He grabbed the vase with a satanic smile. "Are you ready to give up your elf friend?" he asked derisively.

"Where's the sword?" said Paul.

"It's here." Rylan took a few steps and swept away a pile of dead leaves that covered Galton's Sword. He handed it to Paul.

"What can the vase do? Is it really magic?" Rylan asked with curiosity.

"I don't know what it can do. Haralda never told me, but if she says that it has exceptional powers, it must be true. I guess you'll find out."

Paul and Esther exchanged a desperate final glance, before parting from each other. He didn't care about the silver vase anymore. He didn't care that he was never going to make money reselling it. In fact, he didn't even want to find out what magic powers it possessed. In his heart he knew he was leaving the most important person in his life. He grasped Galton's Sword angrily and walked in the direction of his truck, which was parked on a bed of daisies. His next destination was the Royal Palace of Somerville-Langford, where he was going to defeat the sorcerer Moustafa and regain control of the kingdom. Hopefully, he thought, after solving the problem of King James and Prince Richard, Haralda was going to help him retrieve Esther. As he drove through the wood, away from Rylan's castle, the trees began to look shorter and his truck grew taller than the flowers and the blackberry bushes. He was regaining his normal size.

"You will not be the same man and life will seem different to you," Haralda's words echoed in his mind. These were the words that she had pronounced at the Elves' Art Fair. Now he was painfully aware of their significance. Esther had changed his life and his soul. He was no longer Paul Callahan, the selfish merchant who had kept his sister from marrying the man she loved and who had exploited Cedric, his apprentice, for his convenience. He was now a man in love and, like all humans in love, he had discovered self-sacrifice, and suffering as well as happiness. He felt alive and restless. He channeled his efficient organizational skills into his new task, which was to free the Kingdom of Somerville-Langford. However, he wished he could go through this new adventure with Esther. It wasn't fun and exciting without her. He missed her bouncing curls and her pointy elf ears. He missed her groovy skin, her sweet eyes, and her cute little elf boots. He missed her shrewdness and

boldness. He promised himself he would get her back and he would marry her.

He drove all night, zigzagging through the trees, and finally he reached the outskirts of the Kingdom of Somerville-Langford. The kingdom was very large and built along a river. Paul crossed enormous fields of corn and wheat. The farmers' houses seemed large and comfortable, indicating that this kingdom was wealthy and took good care of its people. However, strangely, not one person or animal could be seen anywhere. All window shutters were closed and all barn entrances were barred. As the sun rose, the loud, raspy sound of the crickets filled the silent land. An hour later, he sighted the Royal Palace. Its turrets were studded with precious stones and its walls were decorated with elaborate designs. The palace was surrounded by spectacular gardens and trees heavy with fruit.

Paul parked his truck. He took Galton's Sword and, while he was trying to figure out how to hide it, the sword shrank to the size of a small dagger. *"Everything keeps shrinking!"* he thought, putting the sword into his pocket. A wide stairway made of different types of marble led to the entrance door, which was guarded by two men in armor.

"Who are you? Why aren't you hiding like everybody else?" they asked him.

"I'm not from here. Is there a reason to hide?"

"The cruel sorcerer Moustafa has taken control of the land. King James and Prince Richard are held prisoners in the highest tower," they explained.

"I'm here to free them," Paul said.

The guards eyed him doubtfully, but considering the hopelessness of the situation, they let him in.

"Aren't you afraid like everybody else?"

"No, I'm angry! My best friend has been shrunk and trapped in a magic vase. I have to free the Kingdom of Somerville-Langford before I can save her," Paul explained.

"Hurry! Moustafa is waiting for Rylan the goblin to make King James and Prince Richard disappear," they told him.

"Where's Moustafa?"

"In the spell tower, which used to be the Royal Observatory. Prince Richard is fond of astronomy."

Paul ran up the stairs leading to the spell tower and found Moustafa at a desk, reading a large, old book.

"Why did you lock King James and Prince Richard in the prison tower? I made a deal with Rylan: the royal family was supposed to be banished, but free," Paul confronted him. The Grand Vizier raised his head slowly and stared at him with the dark, narrow slits of his evil eyes.

"Rylan is on his way, as you can see," he said with a sardonic smile on his lips, pointing at the window.

Paul looked out of the window and saw Rylan approaching on a flying carpet. It was a gift that Moustafa had given to him, after being appointed Grand Vizier of Somerville-Langford. Rylan landed gracefully in front of the entrance. Moustafa stood up, clapped his hands twice, and said,

"I'm sole ruler, Grand Vizier
In the prison disappear!"

A white cloud of smoke surrounded Rylan who was no longer visible after the smoke had dissipated.

"I make the deals around here! King James, Prince Richard, and Rylan will share the same fate!" Moustafa said with a deep voice that echoed under the arched ceiling of the spell tower. His long, purple cape, hanging from his wide shoulders, made his figure look tall and menacing. His face was thin and elongated. His pupils were black coals burning in the slits of his eyes. For a split second, Paul thought of Esther and an enormous rage filled his heart. He didn't believe in magic. It was an absurd concept and yet, his life seemed to be controlled by a series of magic events that had overthrown its natural order. He was sure he was not hallucinating. Moustafa the sorcerer, Rylan the goblin, the cruel witches, and Esther--the sweet elf he loved--were all real. He was ready to risk his life for Esther. The world was filled with evil and he, Paul Callahan, a common man with faults and weaknesses, ordinary traits and no particular courage, had been chosen to confront the supernatural forces that were destroying the natural course of life on earth.

He extracted the shrunken Galton's Sword from his pocket. The small dagger turned into a long cutting blade that reflected Moustafa's image. The image grew into a long shadow that curved against the tower ceiling. The sparks of Moustafa's eyes bounced against the walls and back on the sorcerer's body, lighting it on fire. Fear widened his eyes into black pits of fire. Moustafa's dark image, projected onto the ceiling and walls of the tower, slowly enveloped the sorcerer. A dark, distorted shadow slid out of the window and disappeared in the sky, as a horrible scream reverberated inside the castle. Galton's sword magically shrank a second time and Paul put it in his pocket. As an unwilling hero, he walked toward the tallest tower, the prison. Rylan was in a cell adjacent to the cell of King James and Prince Richard.

"Let us out!" King James cried, but Paul ignored his plea, addressing Rylan.

"Where's Esther?"

"In the vase. Almira has it. She lost her goat appearance. If you help me, I'll let you have it," Rylan said.

"Your witches cannot be trusted," Paul objected.

"I'll go with you to Almira's house," Rylan offered.

"No! You'll stay here, while I go to Almira's house," said Paul. He freed King James and Prince Richard.

"Now the kingdom is yours again. Do not release Rylan before I return," he told them.

"Has he lost his powers?" Prince Richard asked.

"Yes, he's under Moustafa's spell."

"As far as I am concerned, he can stay in this tower forever," said King James.

Paul decided to use Rylan's flying carpet, which was outside his cell. It was a very ancient rug, simple in appearance, with burgundy designs, the kind of carpet used by nomadic tribes in the desert.

"Take me to Almira's house!" Paul ordered. Feeling the urgency in his voice, the carpet took off like a fighter jet, performing a few aerobatics in its ride. Paul held on tightly to the corners of the rug, which traveled at supersonic speed, leaving a white stream of vapor behind. He landed in front of Almira's house, a yellow cottage, surrounded by dandelions. He knocked at the door.

"What a surprise! Are you looking for trouble?" she said, opening the door.

"Rylan is in trouble!' he said. Almira's sardonic expression suddenly changed.

"Moustafa double crossed him. Rylan is in jail." Paul explained. Almira grabbed a flying broom next to the door and, as she was about to take off, Paul extracted the shrunken Galton's Sword from his pocket.

"Stop right there! Where's Esther?" he said.

Almira froze at the sight of the sword, which was very powerful, as all witches knew.

"Would you like to give me that sword in exchange for Esther?" she proposed.

"No! I'd like to have Esther or I'll use this sword," Paul threatened her.

"A knight in shining armor!" Almira commented sarcastically.

"You know, I could use my magic and turn you into a frog or a mouse, or maybe shrink you to the size of a pea?" she said.

"No, you can't because I have Galton's Sword," Paul said, hoping that this was true.

"Alright," said the witch. She went into her living room and returned with the silver vase, handing it to him. Esther was beaming with happiness, as she saw Paul, protruding out of the vase. Paul softened for a second at the sight of her unruly curls, quickly regaining his determination.

"Get her out of the vase!" he ordered.

"It's not so simple…" Almira said.

A sunray bounced on the sword and hit Almira who desperately started to gasp for air and fell to the floor, unconscious.

"What a powerful sword!" Esther remarked.

"Is she dead?" asked Paul.

"No, but cut her hair! That's how witches lose their powers" Esther said.

He used the sharp sword to cut Almira's long, white hair. Instantly, Esther rose out of the vase and regained her normal body size. She screamed with joy, jumped up and down, and hugged Paul, who was amazed by the supernatural occurrences that he had produced.

The witch stirred and woke up. As she saw her hair locks on the ground, she began to cry.

"You cut my hair with Galton's Sword! I'll never regain my magic powers, not even when my hair grows back," she said sobbing.

Paul stood in even greater amazement, when he learned that he had just destroyed the magic powers of a witch, although deep in his heart, he still questioned the existence of witches and magic. He placed the sword in his pocket, inevitably shrinking it.

"Let me take you on a dream ride," he proposed, pointing at the magic carpet.

Esther smiled, sitting on the rug next to him. With one hand he was holding the silver vase, which so far, had not exhibited any unusual powers. However, he believed Haralda's words.

"Take us to the royal palace!" he ordered. This time the carpet took off sluggishly, gently gliding through the trees. It was a long, slow ride in which Paul and Esther enjoyed being together. When they reached the royal palace, they immediately climbed the stairs to the jail tower.

"Get me out of here!" Rylan yelled, as soon as he saw them.

Paul hesitated to free him. Suddenly, Rylan began to shrink and was magically pulled into the vase. Paul shook his head in amazement.

"I guess he's trapped!" Esther said. However, she was wrong because a few seconds later, Rylan rose out of the vase and regained his normal size.

"I'm going to shrink you!" the goblin said angrily. He placed his chubby fingers on top of his orange cap and quickly recited the words of a spell:

"I am strong and sly
You are as small as a fly!"

Nothing happened. Rylan repeated the magic words and again nothing happened. He attempted the spell a few more times. Haralda suddenly appeared.

"Rylan, you lost your magic powers in the vase," she explained to him. Rylan began to cry like a little boy.

"I guess he'll have something in common with Almira," said Esther.

"I don't understand…couldn't Rylan have been pulled into the vase sooner?" Paul asked.

"The vase had other goals to accomplish first. If Rylan had been defeated sooner, you and Esther wouldn't have been in this adventure together and you would have never changed," Haralda replied.

"I understand," said Paul. Haralda left, vanishing in her inconspicuous fashion.

"Let's go to my house now. When she sees us arriving on a magic carpet, Rebecca will be thrilled to death!" Paul said laughing.

3

Paul's Wedding

Paul was sitting at the table, feeling particularly cheerful. He had invited Cedric and his wife Gwendolyn as dinner guests. Rebecca had cooked a roast leg of lamb with potatoes. Gwendolyn had brought a delicious cake, layered with vanilla custard, and topped with strawberries and whipped cream.

"I gathered you here tonight to make an official announcement," Paul suddenly said. All eyes were pointed in his direction. "I made a proposal to Esther," he continued, filling his mouth with a large bite of dessert.

"Is it some sort of magic business deal that will take place in the woods?" Cedric asked.

"No, I proposed to her! I'm getting married!" Paul clarified with a smile that did not seem to produce the intended effect.

Rebecca and the two guests dropped their forks, which hit the cake in their plates, splashing whipped cream on their faces.

"Congratulations!" said Gwendolyn, with some reservations. She wasn't fond of the idea of an elf bride, but she was a practical woman and believed that men needed a loving wife to take care of them.

"Are you seriously going to marry one of those creatures?" Rebecca asked.

"They're elves, not creatures," Paul corrected her.

"Are you really in love with an elf?" Rebecca asked, unable to take in the fact that she was going to be related to an elf.

"She's fun, witty, intelligent, kind, and very nice looking," Paul summarized, without gaining real supporters.

As the only male present at this conversation and not blood related, Cedric felt compelled to side up with him.

"She must be a fine elf if Paul wants to marry her," he said.

"Where's the wedding going to take place? In the village or in the woods?" Rebecca inquired with circumspection.

"Neither one. We're going to get married on a field, at the margin of Green Wood, near Clear Creek, where Jarman lives."

"Who is Jarman?" Rebecca inquired.

"He's an old elf, who lives in a tree house, built on the branches of seven oaks, next to Clear Creek. Esther and I estimated that 250 guests will attend the wedding. Therefore, we need a large green space," her brother explained.

"An outdoor wedding is so romantic!" Gwendolyn acknowledged, genuinely.

"How do you plan to have food, chairs, flowers, and everything else, in the middle of a field that is two miles from the village?" Rebecca asked.

Paul thought that Rebecca always worried too much.

"We could use magic catering provided by the wood inhabitants, but I don't really like the idea of magic being present in my wedding," he said, as Rebecca, Cedric, and Gwendolyn stared at him intently. "Therefore, I decided to use Roger's Catering! Roger is one of my grateful customers. I purchased numerous artworks from Rodney, the elf artist, helping Roger furnish his new house with them. He has been extremely satisfied. He'll be happy to supply food, tables, chairs and everything that's needed for the wedding."

"I heard that Roger's Catering isn't very efficient," Cedric objected.

"Nonsense," said Paul.

"What about the honeymoon? Where are you planning to go?" asked Rebecca.

"We'll stay in Captain Sanders' wood cabin, located in Clear Creek. We plan to go fishing, and to relax after our hectic, recent adventures," said Paul, leaving out a small detail.

"That's wonderful!" his audience agreed, relieved by the fact that the cabin belonged to a member of the human community.

Meanwhile, Esther was having dinner at her house, with her sister Wilfreda and Wilfreda's fiancé, the elf Dalbert. As she was about to take her first bite of blueberry pie, Esther announced with a beaming smile, "Paul made a proposal."

"Are you helping him trade some furniture with Rodney?" Wilfreda asked.

"No, he proposed to me! I'm getting married," Esther clarified, still smiling, while her unruly curls bounced on her shoulders.

Both Wilfreda and Dalbert started coughing, as they choked on some blueberry pie they had swallowed too soon. Esther poured some coffee to help them swallow the pie and the news.

"Is that human going to take care of you?" Wilfreda asked.

"He's kind, fun, witty, intelligent, good looking, and we think alike," said Esther.

"Is this wedding going to take place in the woods or in the village?" asked Dalbert.

"Near Jarman's house, next to Clear Creek. We're going to have 250 guests, but no magic catering. Paul doesn't like to have elves and fairies take care of the wedding supplies," Esther explained.

"Then, who is supplying all the food and necessities for such a large crowd?" asked her sister.

"Roger's Catering! Roger is a good customer of Paul."

"Good luck! I heard that he's not very efficient," said Dalbert.

"Who's making your dress?" Wilfreda inquired with resignation.

"Madame Brigitte," Esther replied, referring to the French elf seamstress, who had recently moved into Green Wood.

"Where's he taking you on a honeymoon?" Dalbert continued the interrogation.

"We're going to stay in a cabin that belongs to Captain Sanders. We'll go fishing, and we'll relax near the creek. We're also planning to look for Mordecai's treasure," she replied with excitement in her eyes, adding the detail that Paul had left out.

"Mordecai's treasure?" both Dalbert and Wilfreda repeated with consternation.

"Mordecai trapped over 200 women in his castle. He leaves their bodies in a lifeless state forever. Mordecai is a dangerous sorcerer," Dalbert warned her.

"Nonsense. We're going to have a good time and we're going to find the treasure. It's supposed to be a chest full of gold coins and precious gems. Besides, it doesn't really belong to Mordecai," Esther said, craving action and adventure.

"That's true. The treasure belonged to a very ancient elf that had freed a genie. Mordecai keeps it hidden because, according to the legend, if you find the treasure, you can save the women held captive in his castle," said Dalbert.

The news of Paul's wedding quickly spread across the village, in the neighboring towns, and in Green Wood. On the day of the wedding, over 200 uninvited guests showed up. Roger was faced with a difficult problem, as an insufficient number of chairs had been supplied by his catering service for the regularly invited guests. Now, he needed many more chairs very quickly and no chairs could be located anywhere in the county. Iris the elf fairy, married to Major Montague, and Lodema the witch, who was married to Captain Sanders, increased the number of available chairs with their magic wands. Iris and Lodema wanted to safeguard the success of Paul's wedding because they were two of the few inhabitants of the wood, happily married to humans. Therefore, they also increased the amount of insufficient food, tables, plates, glasses, forks, and other necessities, without Roger realizing it. Regardless of Paul's intentions, Roger's Catering received a significant magic boost.

Paul had invited a very eclectic band of musicians named *The Clinking Coins*. The *Coins* had been instructed to play music that was acceptable to both humans and elves, meaning: German and Italian folk songs for the foreign elves; Irish songs for the local elves and for Paul's family; salsa, merengue, and rock music for everybody; and classical wedding music. When the bandleader, a tall, dark man from South America, named Rafael, saw that the number of guests had spontaneously doubled, he installed all the speakers that he could find in the village. They were not enough. Iris and Lodema magically intervened in their unobtrusive fashion. Rafael was surprised by the good sound projection, in spite of the insufficient number of speakers.

The wedding march elicited a remarkable reaction. The elves whistled, sang, played their foghorns, called the names of the bride and groom, while the humans simply clapped. Esther looked spectacular in her beautiful French wedding dress. A sparkling veil adorned her long curls. She had replaced her usual elves' boots with a pair of satin shoes. Two young elves held the long train of her wedding dress, as she walked among the guests. The butterflies gracefully danced in mid-air as the bride approached. In the front row, Wilfreda and Rebecca were crying desperately. Cedric and Gwendolyn watched with apprehension. They feared that something unforeseen might occur at any moment. Paul looked at Esther, holding his breath. She was a couple of steps away from him when, very suddenly and inexplicably, she disappeared. It took Paul a few seconds to come to the realization that Esther was no longer present. As in a dream, he turned toward the guests, with an empty stare. The guests were also unable to rationalize what had occurred, as they saw Paul standing alone in the wedding aisle. Rafael dramatically stopped the music with a conductor's hand gesture. Wilfreda screamed and fainted. Finally, Paul seemed to rise from his stupor. He turned to his friend Haralda the witch, who was sitting in the front row.

"What happened?" he asked her. Haralda was perplexed.

"I have no idea,"

"Where's Esther?" he pressed her.

"I don't know."

"How can I find her?" he asked with desperation.

"Go to the Spirit of the Well! If you follow the path along the creek for one mile, you'll find an abandoned house and an old well next to it. The spirit who lives inside the well knows almost everything," she said.

Before leaving, Paul used the microphone to address his guests.

"My friends," he said, "I'm going to look for my missing bride." Rebecca also screamed and fainted. "I don't know how long it will take me to find her. The wedding is temporarily postponed.

Please, be patient! I will return as soon as I can." Paul's speech elicited a chaotic reaction. The guests got up from their chairs and began to talk with animation. For the first time, the human villagers and the magic inhabitants of Green Wood seemed to mingle very well, sharing the same curiosity and amazement for the event that had taken place. Wilfreda and Rebecca began to form a family tie, exchanging wild conjectures as to the cause of Esther's disappearance and similar concerns about the rescue mission.

Paul rushed along the path, tripping on a couple of roots, stepping in a small patch of poison ivy, and tearing the sleeve of his suit on a thorny bush. He didn't stop. The smiling image of Esther a few seconds before she vanished was in his mind. He knew that magic had to be involved in her disappearance. He was almost out of breath when he reached the abandoned house. The roof had caved in and, on one side, the wood boards were cracked or missing. In front of the dilapidated house, there was a very old well, made of stones, almost completely covered with ivy. Paul felt a little uncomfortable because speaking with a spirit to find a vanished elf seemed like a very irrational thing to do. However, he was in love with Esther. He had to find her.

He approached the well timidly and peaked inside. It looked like a regular old well, with nothing unusual about it. Yet, he could feel an eerie atmosphere. A lizard ran through the ivy, startling him. He leaned toward the opening and called, "Spirit of the Well! Spirit of the Well!" He heard the voice of a woman, mixed with a gurgling sound.

"Why are you looking for me?"

"I need to talk to you. My fiancée disappeared," was Paul's incoherent answer.

"Lift the bucket!" she said.

Paul grabbed the rope that was holding the bucket and started pulling. The bucket seemed to be stuck.

"Pull harder!" she said.

He pulled harder, pointing his knees against the stones of the well. Suddenly the bucket sprang up and splashed him with water. A loud, cheerful laughter resonated inside the well. *Haralda didn't tell me that this spirit likes to play jokes,* he thought, trying to wipe the water off his face. He leaned toward the opening again.

"Spirit of the Well, I need to talk to you," he repeated.

"All right, drop the bucket and then lift it!"

Paul followed her instructions and, this time, pulling the bucket didn't pose any difficulty. A young, thin woman stepped out of the bucket.

"My name is Evelyn. Sorry I can't shake hands with you: I'm a spirit!" she said and started laughing again.

Paul didn't seem to enjoy her humor and tackled the purpose of his visit.

"My fiancée, an elf named Esther, mysteriously vanished and I don't know where to start looking for her," he said with a grave tone of voice.

"You don't know where she is!" Evelyn exclaimed, with a sardonic smile.

"No, I don't know where she is," Paul repeated, wondering if there was a hidden meaning in her words.

"Well, she's here!" Evelyn told him.

"Here? Where?"

"Right next to you."

"Why isn't she speaking to me?"

"For the same reason that you can't see her."

Paul was totally confused and began to wonder if the Spirit of the Well was crazy.

"Is there any way that you can help me communicate with her?" he asked.

"Talk to her! That's how she can become visible."

"Esther, can you hear me?" Paul said loudly.

"Yes, Paul, I can hear you perfectly well. You don't need to raise your voice," Esther responded, suddenly becoming visible to him. "Why did it take you so long to talk to me?" she asked.

"I never know how to deal with magic. I don't like magic."

"Unfortunately, magic gets in the way sometimes," Evelyn interjected.

Paul tried to hug Esther, but she was immaterial like the Spirit of the Well.

"What exactly happened to her?" he asked Evelyn.

"She's a spirit. Mordecai cast a spell on her."

"What does Mordecai want from Esther?"

"He wants both of you out of this area. He doesn't want you to look for his treasure because he knows that you're a nosy and persistent couple. He never allows anyone too close to his treasure. Did you mention to anyone that you were planning to find Mordecai's treasure?" Evelyn asked.

"Yes," Esther admitted.

"Mordecai has spies everywhere."

"We're happy to leave this area. Is there any way for Esther to regain her body?" Paul asked.

"You have to confront Mordecai," Evelyn said.

The Spirit of the Well stepped into the bucket, vanishing inside the well.

"Good luck!" were her last words.

"We're not leaving this area, Paul!" Esther said.

"Are you trying to cause more trouble?" he started to argue with her.

"Mordecai doesn't know that I'm visible. He thinks that you're still looking for me. Let's use this advantage and find the treasure!" she said.

"We have guests and an organized reception waiting! We'll look for the treasure during our honeymoon, as we had planned," he said.

"No, you forget that I'm a spirit and that we have to go to Mordecai's castle so that I can regain my body. Let's look for the treasure first! Just imagine: an enormous chest full of gold coins and gems!"

He tried to wrap his arm around her, but she was inconsistent. They looked into each other's eyes and felt very sad.

"As an elf, don't you have any special powers that can help in this situation?" he asked her.

"Yes, that's why you can see me, but I cannot reverse a sorcerer's spell" she said. They sat on a rock and began to plan their treasure hunt.

"Where would you hide a chest full of gold coins and gems?" Paul asked.

"I'm an elf. Therefore, I would bury it in the woods, under a tree."

"Do you have a treasure buried in the woods?"

Esther was not comfortable answering this question, because elves considered their gold treasures as very personal possessions. However, since Paul was going to become her husband, she opened up to him.

"Yes, like all elves I collect gold coins and keep them in a pot, hidden under a tree."

"How many gold coins do you have?"

"Not many, as compared to other elves. Only 132."

"132 gold coins? That's a lot of coins, Esther!"

"Jarman has 5,322 coins, or so they say. He's 400 years old and has been collecting them for a long time. No one has ever seen his coins, but they are hidden somewhere," Esther said.

"That's fascinating! What are you going to do with your coins?"

"Nothing!" she answered very abruptly. "They are my personal collection and they are going to stay under the tree, but if you really did need them…I suppose I would give them to you," she said.

"No, I'll never need your coins," he said, understanding the nature of elves.

"Speaking of Jarman, let's go to his house and ask him how we can find Mordecai's treasure," Esther suggested.

They walked to Jarman's house, which was an enormous structure consisting of numerous units, built on the branches of different trees. The units were connected with bridges and rope ladders. Paul knocked at the door, which means that he hit the large pan hanging from a tree branch, using the hammer that was in front of the entrance door. The loud gong attracted Jarman's attention.

"I'll be right there!" he yelled from the fifth level of a distant tree. He used ropes to swing from one branch to another and walked down some ladders, eventually reaching the tree on which the entrance unit was built.

"Good Heavens!" he exclaimed, when he saw that Esther had been turned into a spirit. Paul briefed him on the recent developments.

"Where could we possibly find this treasure?" he asked Jarman.

"If you really want me to help you pursue this mad treasure hunt, we have to go to my storehouse, on the second floor. That's where I keep my magic gem collection,"

Jarman said, leading the way. They climbed a rope ladder and used a second rope to swing to another tree. Next to Jarman's library was a large room full of stones, from different parts of the world. They had different colors and dimensions. Pointing at a locked cabinet, Jarman said, "My magic gems are in there." He extracted a key from his pocket and opened the cabinet, revealing a set of small gems that radiated with a brilliant light. He picked one up. It was pink, with an elongated, hexagonal shape.

"Magic tourmaline," Jarman said, handing it to Paul. "If you look into it, you'll see clues that will help you find Mordecai's treasure," Jarman explained. Paul and Esther stared into the crystal and gradually saw some blue swirls that looked like flowing water. Next to the blue swirls, they saw a round green shape and some red spots near an irregular brown structure.

"Clear Creek! That's the well covered with green ivy and the red poppies near the abandoned house!" the couple said excitedly.

"Before you go, I have a gift for you," Jarman said. He picked up another magic stone, which was yellow, "This is a special golden beryl. Esther, if you stare into it, you'll regain your body."

"I thought that no one could reverse Mordecai's spells, except for Mordecai?" Paul interjected.

"The spell can't be reversed if it's cast on a human. Since Esther is an elf, my magic gem will work!" Jarman explained.

Esther looked into the yellow crystal and, for a few seconds, she seemed to be surrounded by a golden aura. When she was able to touch and hold the magic gem, she was no longer immaterial. She hugged both Paul and Jarman. Still unable to sort out in his mind what had just happened, Paul shook hands with Jarman.

"I have one favor to ask you. I cannot go on a treasure hunt in my wedding dress. Is there any way that you could help me change my outfit?" Esther asked Jarman.

"Sure, I have a magic rose of the desert that can help you. Close your eyes, touch it with both hands, and imagine what you would like to wear," he instructed her. Esther placed her hands on the scaly rock and closed her eyes. When she opened her eyes, she was wearing her everyday flowery dress, her pointed hat, and elf boots.

"Where's my wedding dress?" she asked.

"It's right here, on that table. It didn't disappear. Good luck! You're a stubborn couple!" said Jarman.

"I'll be back to retrieve my wedding dress!" said Esther, waving goodbye.

Paul and Esther followed Clear Creek in the direction they had come from, and soon reached the old well. As they were walking toward the house, they heard Evelyn's voice crying inside the well:

"Help me! Help me! Lift the bucket!" Paul and Esther grabbed the rope and pulled. The bucket came up slowly. The voice became gradually louder.

"I'm a little heavy. Don't stop pulling!" Suddenly the bucket sprang up, splashing the couple with water. Evelyn's laughter echoed inside the well. Paul realized that the Spirit of the Well had played one of her jokes on them. Slightly annoyed, he and Esther wiped the water off their faces. They walked in the direction of the abandoned house, which was surrounded by overgrown weeds and poppies.

"Where do you think the treasure could be hidden?" Esther asked.

"Maybe it's in one of the rooms," he said. However, they couldn't find any trace of it, although they inspected every corner of the house.

"Mordecai isn't going to keep his treasure in a room where everyone can see it," Esther rationalized.

"It must be behind one of the walls," Paul concluded.

"Behind a wall? What does that mean?"

"Haven't you ever seen a sliding wall or a wall that can turn and reveal another room behind it?"

"Of course! But how are we going to find the spot that slides and turns?" Esther asked.

"You're an elf. You should be able to feel the presence of a treasure! Can't you just feel where the coins are in the house? Concentrate!" he urged her.

Esther tried to visualize an enormous chest full of gold coins and gems, as she slowly walked through the house. With her groovy hands, she touched the walls and tried to feel some vibrations that would indicate the presence of the chest. Gradually, her elfish nature took control of her. She moved through the house like a hound after its prey. A mysterious force drove her to the second floor. She entered the study and felt compelled to examine one of its walls. Her hands started to shake and her heart beat faster. She paused, as her hands touched the wall above the fireplace. She looked at Paul smiling.

"It's behind this wall, isn't it?"

"Yes," she said. She inspected the entire fireplace until one of its bricks made a slight movement, and the wall began to rotate. The couple entered the room and gasped. An enormous chest, much bigger than they had imagined, was overfilled with gold coins and sparkling gems of all shapes and sizes. Like all elves do in front of a treasure, Esther screamed happily and danced, kicking her feet up and down, jumping, and pirouetting. Paul watched her, amused. He also felt excitement for this incredible find, and yet a feeling of uneasiness began to grow inside of him. This enormous treasure had belonged to an elf, which meant that it was a magic treasure. Now it belonged, rightfully or not, to an evil sorcerer. Taking possession of it couldn't be a simple task.

"What do we do with this treasure?" Paul asked.

"First, we hide it, then we save the women in Mordecai's castle, and then we share it with all the elves. It's an elf treasure," Esther said, not noticing the serious expression on Paul's face.

"How do we hide something this big?"

"The way elves do: underground!"

"Esther, it will take us a lifetime to carry the contents of this chest outside."

"We can take the treasure outside, by channeling it through a window. Then, we bury it."

"Channeling it? How?"

"With pipes! The house is full of pipes."

Paul didn't want to question the feasibility of this plan, as he already had given up on understanding elf logic. He went to look for pipes with her. They raised cracked boards in various parts of the house, collecting eight pipes. They connected these pipes in a way that they led down to the first floor, but they weren't sufficient in number to reach a window.

"There are no more pipes that we can use," he said.

"We'll have to find a hollow tree trunk," she said.

The fog was beginning to condense in the air. The day had turned to dusk. A few stars appeared in the sky, but thick clouds were quickly moving in. The screech of a bird cut through the wood like a knife. They saw a fire in the distance.

"It's probably a witch," Esther said, holding Paul's hand and shaking a little.

"Are you sure that we should take the treasure?" he asked.

"We must save the women in Mordecai's castle," she replied. Paul resigned himself to the role of benefactor because he loved Esther and, in spite of the dangers involved, he was enjoying himself in this new adventure.

"How do we find a hollow tree in the fog?" he asked.

"Let's ask the Spirit of the Well."

They walked toward the well. The ivy looked pitch-black. They leaned over the opening, but couldn't see the water inside.

"Spirit of the Well! Evelyn!" Paul called.

"What do you want at this hour of the night?"

"I'd like to ask you a question."

"Lift the bucket!"

"No! I won't lift the bucket!" he said decisively.

"Do as you wish. I'm going back to sleep," said Evelyn.

"We need your help!" he insisted. He picked up a few rocks and started throwing them into the well.

"I'll fill the well if you don't come out of there!" he said. Esther also started picking up pebbles, pieces of wood, acorns, and a few rotten apples she found under a tree. Together they began bombarding the well. A splash of water soaked them. However, they didn't stop their attack and continued to throw objects into the opening. Esther unloaded a large amount of dirt she collected with her elf hat. Evelyn screamed and slowly began to rise to the top, with acorns in her hair and dirt covering her face. For a split second, Paul questioned how material objects, like acorns, could remain entangled in a spirit's hair curls, but he immediately decided to interrupt a reasoning process that wouldn't have led to a logical answer.

"Stop polluting my well! What do you need to ask me at this hour of the night?" Evelyn said, coughing and spitting dirt out of her mouth.

"We're looking for a hollow tree trunk, but we can't find one in the dark."

"The closest hollow trunk is in the back of the house. There should be an axe in front of the house. Be careful, Mordecai is more powerful than you think! I suggest that you keep a red-orange ruby and take it to the castle." Evelyn retreated inside the well and disappeared.

Paul and Esther found the axe and also a shovel next to it. They located the hollow trunk, cut a long piece off, and connected it to the last pipe. Then, they ran upstairs and searched through the gems, which were visible because they shone in the darkness.

"Found it!" said Esther, as she picked a red-orange ruby and put it in her pocket. They started scooping gems and coins into the pipes. The treasure rolled down and out of the window. It took an hour to empty the chest. The couple ran outside. The treasure was a dazzling spectacle on the ground. They sat on it to rest. The clouds opened up, allowing the moonlight to shine over it. The gems looked like colorful sparks of fire. The coins were as bright as golden flames. For a moment, Paul considered how strange it was for him to be in the woods at night, next to an elf, sitting on a large treasure. He looked at Esther, whose facial expression showed satisfaction for the difficult task they had accomplished. He felt lucky to be with her. He looked at the treasure that he would have had to give to the elves, as it belonged to them, and he thought that he really didn't care about the coins and the gems as much as he cared for his new life.

"What are you thinking?" she asked him.

"I was thinking that life is about doing things. You get up in the morning and you start doing things, all sorts of things. Some are tedious, some are fun, some are necessary for survival, some are imposed, and some are chosen. That's what life is about, no matter how intellectual we try to be. We never stop doing things, day after day, but this… this is the most incredible type of life I could have ever imagined and you are part of it. You'll always be part of my life, Esther," he said. They hugged on top of the treasure, alone in the woods, and yet in harmony with the universe.

They got up and took a few steps to get the shovel, but when they returned, there was no trace of the treasure. It had vanished completely. Esther and Paul were speechless. They stared at the spot where only a couple of minutes earlier a large number of coins and gems lay in the moonlight. Paul was certain that he hadn't imagined the treasure. He knew he had seen it and touched it. Now, it was no longer there. Reality and imagination seemed to be constantly overlapping. He looked at Esther and touched her. She was real, material, present. The trees were also real, the moon was always the same moon he had known since he had been a child. The smell of moss was strong, undeniable. The breeze felt sharp on his face. Who was Paul Callahan? Where was he? Was he living a dream or was he truly the protagonist of a story that was as fascinating as poignant?

"Let's go to Mordecai's castle," Esther said, stirring him from his introspection. From a tree branch, the round eyes of an owl followed the outline of a tall man and a short elf, walking in the night.

The gate of Mordecai's property was open. As they entered his property, they were amazed to see the large number of orange trees that surrounded the castle. Esther knew that each orange was connected to the life of one of the women, held captive in the castle.

"I heard that it is possible to revive each captive woman by placing the right orange on her heart. Each woman has a matching ghostly image, moving inside the castle, which has to be reunited with its lifeless body," she told Paul.

They couldn't save over 200 women easily. It would have been impossible to identify the right orange for each lifeless woman. As they entered the castle, the women's ghostly images were dancing with the magic images of men, in the ballroom. Their eyes had a dream-like quality. The figures moved lightly and noiselessly, while soft music filled the room.

"What do you say if we dance while we wait for Mordecai?" Paul proposed.

Esther accepted. For a couple of hours, they enjoyed themselves and almost forgot the purpose of their visit. Suddenly an explosion brought them back to reality. It was Mordecai's spectacular entrance. He materialized from the smoke, right in front of them, interrupting their dance.

"We have a couple of intruders! If you're here for the treasure, it's too late: I hid it," said Mordecai.

"Are you afraid that we may use the treasure to interfere with your spell?" Esther confronted him boldly.

"I'm not afraid of you and since you like my castle, you can stay in it forever!" He quickly covered her face with his gold cape and whispered some magic words. Esther fell to the floor, remaining motionless. At the same time, Esther's ghostly image detached itself from her body and took a few uncertain steps, like a sleepwalker.

"I'll keep her soul together with your sister's soul!" Mordecai told Paul.

"What? My sister's soul?" Paul repeated with sudden apprehension.

Mordecai quickly moved away, through the crowd of ghosts, and returned holding the arm of Rebecca's ghost. Mordecai smiled mockingly and left. Esther's and Rebecca's ghostly images didn't seem to recognize each other.

"Esther! Esther!" Paul called with a tone of despair. She didn't seem to hear him.

"Rebecca! Rebecca!" another voice called his sister. He turned and, with astonishment, saw David, the town baker. Rebecca's ghost was moving aimlessly, without responding to the calls. Heavy tears rolled down David's face.

"What happened to her?" he asked Paul.

"The sorcerer Mordecai is holding her captive, like Esther. How did you find this place?"

"One of your wedding guests, named Haralda, showed up in my bakery. She told me that Rebecca had vanished and was under a magic spell. She said that she was a witch and that I could rescue Rebecca if I came here," David vocalized somewhat incoherently. Paul felt a sharp pang of guilt for not having invited David to his wedding.

"I love Rebecca!" David confessed with tears in his eyes.

Paul felt ashamed for having separated David and Rebecca.

"Please forgive me!" he told David, who completely ignored his words.

"What exactly happened to her?" David asked.

"The sorcerer Mordecai left her body lifeless, detaching her soul, which walks around like a ghost. He cast his spell on 200 women, including Esther," Paul said pointing at Esther's body, lying on the floor.

"I have to find Rebecca. Haralda said that I can revive her by placing an orange on her heart," said David.

"It's not that simple!" said Paul. "You have to match the right orange with the right woman. However, let's look for Rebecca's body". The two men searched the entire castle. They rushed through hallways, opened doors, climbed stairs, inspected turrets, encountering lifeless women everywhere, but there was no trace of Rebecca.

"Did Haralda give you any indication?" asked Paul.

"She only said, *Check inside and outside the castle!*"

"Outside the castle? What are we waiting for?"

They rushed out of the front door and, behind the castle, they inspected the garden. There were inert women on the benches, in the gazebo, and on the flower beds.

"Near the fountain! That's Rebecca!" Paul screamed, recognizing his sister's clothes. David kneeled on the ground next to her.

"Bring her to the orchard, on the other side of the castle! I'm going to get Esther. We'll meet there," said Paul. A few minutes later, as he reached the orchard holding Esther in his arms, Paul found David completely distraught. His eyes were the eyes of a bull that had been stabbed in the heart. David raised his face toward the starry sky and shouted. His cry of despair traveled through space, echoing in a timeless dimension. His voice had lost its human quality. It was the sound of a rushing river during a flood, of a house crushed by an avalanche, of a tree parched by magma. His agonizing cry subsided. He hugged Rebecca and wept quietly. Paul recognized his own suffering. He placed Esther on the ground, next to Rebecca. The two most important women in his life, his closest family members, were lifeless. He stood, motionless, not knowing what to do. Time had stopped for him as well.

Chloe, the tree fairy, in the form of a nightingale, sang, perched on an orange tree. He didn't hear her. Chloe assumed her human form and walked close to him. She was a little female figure, wearing a long pink tunic.

"Paul!" she called him, with a gentle voice. He opened his eyes and looked at her through his tears.

"You can bring Esther back."

"She's gone," he said mechanically. "How could I possibly find the right orange among hundreds of oranges? Besides I'm sure that Mordecai cast a spell that cannot be reversed with a simple orange," he said angrily.

"Look in Esther's pocket. The orange-red ruby!" He searched her pockets and found the brilliant gem. It felt warm in his hand.

"Go back inside and confront Mordecai!" she told him.

Paul slowly got up and robotically entered the ballroom. He found Mordecai dancing with Esther's ghost. Anger and pain drove Paul like a fury. There is nothing more powerful than hatred mixed with love in a man's heart.

"Leave her!" he roared. The light of the chandelier ignited the magic gem he was still holding with his hand. Its red-orange sparkle was reflected on Mordecai, who began to shrivel. He was wrapped in his cape and was blown into the sky by the force of the gem. It flew high, over the trees and into the clouds.

"Is he gone forever?" Paul asked Chloe.

"Yes. His evil nature destroyed him. Unfortunately, evil exists, and when it becomes overwhelming it's self-destructive. The magic gem was the medium that brought order back into life, but without you Paul, this wouldn't have been possible. Your emotional drive empowered the gem." Chloe turned into a nightingale and flew away. David had watched the extraordinary sorcerer's annihilation in astonishment.

Paul placed the gem on Esther's heart and said, "Please come back, I need you." Her ghostly image approached timidly and reentered her body. Esther blinked several times, reviving from her lifeless state. Her face lost its pallor. Then, Paul gave the gem to David, who placed it on Rebecca's heart and said, "I can't live without you, Rebecca. Please come back!" Rebecca's ghost approached and was reunited with her body.

"Where am I?" Rebecca whispered, as she opened her eyes.

"You're in Mordecai's castle. The sorcerer Mordecai had trapped you and Esther in his castle. David saved you," explained Paul. While he was talking, an orange fell on his head. It seemed extremely heavy, like a small boulder. Numerous other oranges started falling. One after another, all the oranges of the orchard fell heavily to the ground, rolling and bouncing in all directions, each stopping on the heart of a lifeless woman. All women were reunited with their ghostly images, gaining vitality. It was time for them to go back to their life and their family.

"How did you know I was here?" Rebecca asked David.

"Haralda the witch, one of Paul's wedding guests, came to my bakery and told me what had happened to you. I immediately shut down my bakery and came to your rescue." She understood that he deeply cared for her and was very happy.

"I hope that you will continue to look after my sister," Paul told him.

"You can count on it!"

"Would you please be the best man at my wedding?" Paul asked him.

"Gladly!" David and Paul shook hands, sealing the beginning of a friendship that was going to last a lifetime.

"We'll see you at the wedding as soon as possible," said Paul.

"Why aren't you going to the wedding now?" asked Rebecca with wariness.

"We still have to retrieve Esther's wedding dress at Jarman's house," said Paul.

As soon as Rebecca and David left, Esther said, "We haven't found Mordecai's treasure yet."

"I was hoping you would say that!" Paul smiled with satisfaction. He liked her obstinacy.

"Where could the treasure be?" she pondered.

"There's only one place," he said, rubbing his head, where he had been hit by the orange. Esther screamed like an elf. She picked up an orange, opened it, and found inside a handful of gems and coins.

"The treasure is in the oranges!" Esther acknowledged.

"Let's go to our wedding and then tell the elves to come and collect their share of the treasure," said Paul.

"Take half of my orange," Esther offered.

"No, I don't want part of your share of the treasure. That's for your gold pot. However, I do want to keep the ruby that brought you back to life," said Paul.

"What are you going to do with it?"

"I'm going to start my own gold pot! I will cherish that gem forever!" he said.

They walked toward Jarman's house to retrieve Esther's wedding dress. Deep in the night, the round eyes of an owl followed a man and a woman, happily walking through the woods, ready to start their married life together.

4

The Frog from Hell

When Paul and Esther returned to their wedding site, they were greeted with loud cheering, clapping, and whistling for thirty minutes. The ceremony took place without any problems and the reception was an international success. Uninvited elves from Italy, Germany, France, Spain, and other countries showed up after the news of Esther's disappearance had spread internationally. They interacted with the human community, enjoying themselves. The *Clinking Coins* kept the entire crowd on the dance floor for most of the night. The elves, in particular, danced wildly, as they learned that they were going to receive a share of the recovered treasure.

"Take good care of the shop! I'll be back in a week," were Paul's last words to Cedric, before leaving for his honeymoon. The following morning, punctual as usual, Cedric entered Paul's shop to begin his day of work. As he was checking a porcelain tureen, his mind wandered and, for a few seconds, he thought about a delicious cream of mushroom soup. He could almost smell it, taste it, and even feel its warm steam spreading through the air. He removed the lid and was rudely brought back to reality. A large, green, warty frog jumped out of the tureen, nearly giving him a heart attack. For a second, the image of the cream of mushroom soup was replaced in his mind by the less appealing one of frog legs, in a buttery Provençal sauce.

"Thank goodness! I was getting claustrophobic!" the frog said. Cedric eyed it with concern.

"You're not…a princess, by any chance, are you?" he asked.

"A princess? No! Do I look like a princess?" said the frog. Cedric sighed with relief, but in his heart, he knew that this was not going to be a simple encounter and decided to shorten it. He opened the front door and said, "You're welcome to go outside. It's a beautiful day."

"Don't you want to ask me who I am?" said the frog.

"I don't want to pry into other people's business and I'm sure that you have a very busy day ahead, out there…wherever frogs go."

"*People* is the right word because I'm not a real frog, since I'm able to speak." For the second time, Cedric avoided questioning the identity of the frog. He just wanted to move on with his work and prevent the type of unpleasant situations that had been occurring in Paul's shop lately.

"All right, since you don't want to ask me who I am, I'll tell you that you're my master," the frog continued.

"You're a genie!" Cedric exclaimed without enthusiasm.

"I'm not a genie. I'm a witch that was turned into a frog and you own me, like a pet dog."

"That kind of master!" Cedric said, with a worried expression on his face. "Do I get any wishes?"

"I'm not a genie!" the frog repeated. "My name is Cornelia. I'm an evil witch. Lodema turned me into a frog."

"What do you normally look like?"

"Normally I look like an ugly, warty witch, with a slightly green complexion; the typical mean witch with a long nose, a long chin, and wiry hair, wearing ragged clothes," the frog answered with satisfaction.

"Since I'm your master, I order you to leave now! Shoo! Shoo!" Cedric said, grabbing a broom and pushing the frog toward the front door with repeated sweeping strokes. The frog jumped and exhaled a flame from its mouth, which charred the broom bristles. Cedric was petrified.

"When I say that you're my master, I don't mean that you can order me around. Your role is to help me recover my identity."

"How?" Cedric asked, resigned to his new role of master attendant.

"Lodema will let me regain my identity when I do something good, like helping someone in need. You must help me find someone who needs my help. I've never been good and I don't know how to even start," the frog said.

Cedric had many things to do, but he thought it would be better to get Cornelia's business out of the way first. It was not wise to have a witch in the shop, regardless of her outer appearance.

"Let's walk to the bakery. David Rosen always knows what's happening in town," Cedric said.

"All right, but I'm not planning to hop all the way there." Cornelia exhaled a green breath of air over the broom, instantly shrinking it. Then she hopped on the tiny broom, and moved off the ground.

"I'll fly next to you," she said.

Cedric was not happy. His day of work had been ruined. He had been unwillingly recruited to be part of an adventure that surely involved magic. He took a few steps out of the shop, followed by the frog flying at a very slow speed. He was so deeply absorbed in his unhappy thoughts that he almost collided with Rebecca,

Paul's sister. She was astonished to see the frog flying on the small broom.

"Are you together?" she asked.

"Yes, I'm the attendant of this frog named Cornelia, under the pretense of being her master," said Cedric. "We're looking for someone who needs help. If Cornelia does a good deed, Lodema the witch will restore her real identity and I can be free," Cedric explained, omitting to disclose the fact that the frog was a witch.

"David needs help!" said Rebecca.

"Did something happen to him?"

"Yes, since yesterday, his cakes don't rise, his custards curdle, his bread loaves burn, and his caramels crystallize."

"Interesting. What exactly happened yesterday?" Cornelia asked.

"A customer wanted a strudel that had been reserved for Dr. Dillingham. David refused to sell it to him and the man cursed the bakery." Rebecca started to cry.

"What did he look like?" Cornelia asked.

"David says that he was tall, dark, and that he was wearing a long brocade jacket."

"It can only be Osmar the sorcerer!" said the frog.

"Osmar the sorcerer? I heard that he's mad," Cedric said.

"Yes, he's crazy and out of control when he uses his powers," said Cornelia. Cedric and Cornelia were suddenly aware of Rebecca's desperate sobs.

"Let's go to the bakery and see what Cornelia can do to help David," Cedric tried to comfort her. As they started walking in the direction of the bakery, Cornelia took off, leaving a trail of black smoke behind. Her little broom joined a flock of geese flying together in a "V" formation. Cornelia seemed to be enjoying herself, as she coordinated her movement with that of the flock. She lowered her frog head slightly toward the broomstick and adjusted her body position to the swooping motion of the broom, synchronized with the flight of the geese. Rebecca stopped crying, as she watched the little broom flying like a jet in an air show. David Rosen's bakery became visible between a newspaper shop and a small hardware store. A *Closed* sign was hung on the entrance door. A small crowd of people stood in front of the bakery, holding an animated discussion as to the possible reasons for the sign.

"I need to buy a cake for my daughter's birthday party!" "I need bread for dinner!" "My husband wants pastries!" "Why is the bakery closed today?" they questioned Rebecca. She stared at them quietly, as tears began to roll down her face again.

"Witchcraft!" Cedric voiced sternly. Everyone gasped. Right at that moment, the frog on the little broom gracefully circled the small crowd and stopped in mid-air, next to Cedric.

"Is Rebecca going to open the door?" Cornelia asked.

"A talking frog!" a woman gasped in horror. Someone screamed.

"The place is controlled by some evil sorcery!" Within a few seconds, all the people standing in front of the bakery left. Rebecca opened the door. Cedric stepped into the shop, followed by Cornelia on her broom. The pastry cases in the front room were completely empty. They entered the kitchen, where they found David sitting on a stool, next to a tray, filled with flattened puffs.

"I'm ruined," he mumbled.

"We're here to help. Let me introduce Cornelia. She's a good witch…"

Cornelia interrupted Cedric with a loud croak, eyeing him disapprovingly, while Rebecca watched with apprehension.

"…I mean, Cornelia is a mean witch who has to do a good action in order to regain her natural appearance. Lodema turned her into a frog."

"Can you reverse the spell on my bakery?" David asked Cornelia.

"Yes, with another magic spell," she said, dismounting her broom.

"What are we waiting for?" Rebecca interjected.

"It's not as easy as it sounds. We have to go to my spell room and you have to help me because I can't even add magic ingredients into the cauldron, in my present amphibian state."

"We'll be happy to follow your directions. Let's rush to your spell room!" Cedric said, hoping to solve the problem quickly and return to the shop he had left unattended.

Cornelia seemed to hesitate.

"Is there something else?" Cedric asked.

"Yes…my spell room is not exactly in a blissful place…you may not like to go there," she said in one hurried, green breath that turned the flat puffs on the tray into a pile of dust.

"Nonsense! We've had some experience with magic before," Cedric said. Cornelia stared at them for a few seconds, squinting her bulbous, orange eyes. The three humans stared back at her in desperate anticipation.

"Fine! Come with me and don't complain if you don't like my spell room." They were ready to follow the frog to hell, in order to save the bakery.

"Just a minute…before we go…" Cornelia said, stalling again. She hopped into the sink and dove into a large bowl, filled with water. She rolled a couple of times underwater. Then she emerged, producing a gurgling sound with her throat. She kicked her hind legs, beginning to swim around the improvised pond, splashing water out of the sink. Cedric wiped his face, but didn't have the courage to interrupt her. She croaked, gently rolling on her back and floating on the water. Then, she jumped in and out of the bowl a few times, producing big, bright, purple bubbles of air that slowly moved over the bowl. One of them reached Cedric's nose and popped into a colorful explosion of sparks. The three friends stared dumbfounded.

"Cornelia, we have to go!" finally Cedric said with urgency.

"All right, all right!" she hopped out of the bowl, shaking like a shaggy dog after its bath. She mounted her tiny broom and led the way.

The three humans walked away from the village and into the woods, following the flying witch. The beds of moss and patches of grass among the trees became smaller and smaller. The tree branches grew thicker and wider. They stepped carefully over large roots, trying to make their way through the foliage, while Cornelia zigzagged between tall plants, occasionally colliding with a large leaf or a flower full of pollen. She sneezed a couple of times, as the pollen spread around her in a sparkling cloud. Rebecca held David's hand tightly.

"I've never been to a witch house," she whispered in his ear.

"Don't worry: we are guests and Cornelia needs us as much as we need her," he reassured her.

"This part of the wood is very dark," Cedric said, realizing that they were alone in the middle of a thick forest.

"That's right. None of the elves live here," Cornelia said, while her orange eyes seemed to glow. Rebecca shivered. A thin, grey fog began to spread among the trees. The air turned cold. It was a moonless evening.

"That's my house!" Cornelia said, pointing at a black gothic style construction, completely engulfed by the trees, and barely visible in the dusk. As they approached the entrance, the trees swayed their twisted branches into convoluted shapes, moaning and screeching. One of the branches barred the way. Cedric, who was in front of David and Rebecca, unsuccessfully tried to move the massive branch. He bent forward trying to slide under it, but other branches moved downwards, blocking his way. David and Rebecca attempted a different route, with the same result. A chorus of moans and howls echoed in the night. They heard a soft hissing sound coming from the large branch that was blocking Cedric's way. The sound gradually turned into a whisper that played the same words over and over.

"Staaaaaay awaaaaaay! Staaaaaay awaaaaaay..."

"Cornelia, are your trees possessed?" Cedric shouted.

Cornelia replied with a very loud cackle that reverberated inside her throat. Cedric stared at her black outline against the grey background of the sky. She seemed to have grown into a very large toad.

"They're inhabited..." she finally replied with aloofness.

"By whom?" David, Rebecca, and Cedric asked simultaneously. Cornelia blinked a couple of times.

"They're inhabited by creatures of the wood," was her vague answer.

"You mean squirrels or birds?" David said.

"No, no, squirrels and birds can't speak. I mean speaking creatures."

"Humans?" Cedric asked in horror.

"No, not humans..." Cornelia hesitated, while her eyes turned a dark shade of orange, reminiscent of a sunset.

"What kind of creatures did you trap in these trees?" Cedric asked.

"Just elves."

"Elves?" Rebecca repeated in dismay. She never felt comfortable acknowledging the existence of elves, but since her brother had married an elf, she felt the compelling need to side with the elf community. Esther and Wilfreda belonged to her family now and family members were supposed to stick together. As Rebecca was sorting out her conflicting feelings towards elves, Cornelia expressed her animosity towards these little creatures of the wood.

"Yes, some cocky, annoying, nosy elves who shouldn't have walked through this side of the wood."

"No wonder Lodema turned you into a frog!" Cedric said. A background of whispers rose from the trees in assent.

"How many?" David asked.

"I don't know…four, maybe six or seven, I can't remember. What difference does it make?"

"You must free them!"

Cornelia flew in front of Cedric, confronting him with an evil, orange stare.

"If you weren't my master, I would trap you into that tall eucalyptus, right behind you!" she said with a low tone of voice, at the same time exhaling a breath of air that formed green spirals in the mist. Rebecca screamed. Cedric was not taken aback.

"You must free these elves before you solve David's problem! If you don't, Lodema will not let you regain your human form."

"Lodema said that I had to do one good action, not become the champion of good. Solving David's problem is all I need to regain my human form or, perhaps, I could just free the elves."

"You need to be a good Samaritan and help someone in need," Cedric said.

"Do I really need to free the elves in addition to helping David?" Cornelia asked, exhaling a little flame that annihilated a caterpillar, sprawled out on a tree branch in front of her. She had the impression that too much good was expected of her. Helping others was not in her nature.

"If you don't free the elves, we won't help you in the spell room," Rebecca added coldly.

"That's right!" said David.

"I agree!" Cedric said, joining the elves' cause.

"Very well…I shall free them…but this won't prevent me from trapping other elves in the future. I don't like those little, wrinkled creatures, tiptoeing around my house, peeking into my windows, and climbing on my roof. They are nosy and interfere with my spells by adding ingredients into my cauldron when I am not watching."

A loud moan echoed among the tree branches. Cornelia flew above the tall eucalyptus tree. She touched it with one of her toes, at the same time exhaling a pink breath that circled the tree like a ring of smoke. The tree produced a snapping sound and opened its trunk to release a shivering elf. Cornelia flew to the next tree, repeating the ritual and freeing a second elf. She stopped when she had freed 29 elves.

"Six or seven!" Cedric exclaimed indignantly, while Cornelia looked at him with an innocent expression. Her eyes were a pale orange color, tinged with gold. She flew on top of the eucalyptus tree and glancing at the fleeing elves, she addressed them with her hoarse voice:

"Run away, very, very fast, evil spirits won't let you rest!"

The elves screamed as a crowd of dark, ghostly figures, coming from all directions, began to chase them.

"Freeing the elves and then sending evil spirits to chase after them definitely doesn't count as a Samaritan action," Cedric commented with disapproval.

"I gave them a good scare!" Cornelia cackled in the night.

"You must stop defying Lodema with your evil ways or you'll be a frog forever," Cedric warned her.

A cold breeze embraced the group. It was time to go inside Cornelia's manor, which looked like a haunted house. A red lantern in the front porch created a spooky atmosphere. Skulls were carved into the front door. Thick cobwebs covered the walls. An old, skeletal man greeted them at the entrance.

"Good evening, Lady Cornelia. I see that you still haven't regained your normal form."

"Hello Holbrook! Hopefully, after tonight's spell, I'll be myself again."

The butler led them into the living room, brightened by the flames of a fireplace. In front of the fire, four black armchairs surrounded a mahogany coffee table.

"Please, have a seat. I'll get some sherry," he said, walking out of the room with the robotic gait of a zombie.

"Is he alive?" Cedric asked, eyeing Holbrook with suspicion.

"Oh yes. He's just very old. I lengthened his life. I couldn't afford to lose him. He has been in my service for 167 years," said Cornelia. The witch dismounted her broom on top of the coffee table, clearly feeling uncomfortable because of the dry heat of the fireplace.

Holbrook returned with a tray. He placed on the table a bowl, filled with water and some rose petals, and three empty glasses. While Cornelia hopped into the bowl, Holbrook poured sherry into the glasses. The fireplace projected black shadows on the walls. They looked like monstrous figures with red eyes. Unusual swishing and howling sounds mixed with the crackling of the logs in the fireplace. The window shutters banged periodically, shaking the glass chandelier. Holbrook stood in a corner, looking like a tall, white, fleshless figure from the underworld. The three human guests swallowed their sherry in one gulp, unsuccessfully trying to relieve their tension.

"Shall we go to the spell room?" David suggested.

"Ready! I want my regular skin back," the frog said, emerging from underwater. She hopped out of the bowl and mounted her broom again. She led her human guests through a long hallway, barely lit by candlelight. They began to climb a spiral staircase. The banister was made of wrought iron and seemed to be hot to the touch. In the center of the spiral staircase, the image of a young woman appeared and disappeared. She had dark circles around her eyes. Rebecca screamed every time her image became visible. David, also perturbed, held Rebecca with both arms, helping her climb the stairs. Even Cedric seemed very uncomfortable as he followed them, step after step.

"Who's that woman?" David asked.

"That's the ghost of Lady Rosabel, one of Osmar's victims. She died six months ago."

"Osmar imprisoned her in his castle, where she died. She'll be a wandering ghost forever."

"That's horrible!" said Rebecca.

"Osmar is a crazy sorcerer."

"How long is this staircase?" Cedric asked, as the stairs seemed to wind endlessly ahead.

"It's a tall tower," said Cornelia. A ghost, dressed in a tuxedo, replaced the image of Lady Rosabel. He looked like a young man with a bleeding wound on his head. He stared at Cedric insistently, while the corners of his mouth curved into an evil grin.

"What do you want?" Cedric mumbled.

"I want to borrow your body. I want to be able to run, eat, drink, dance, and do all the things that I used to do when I was alive."

"Can't you do all that as a ghost?"

"No, I can't touch or hold anything with my hands. My body is only an illusion."

"I can't give my body to you. I need it!" Cedric said.

"Hi, Roger! Cedric is with me. Find another body elsewhere!" Cornelia said. She exhaled a blue breath of air that surrounded the ghost, who froze into a statue.

"If he gets hold of a body, he won't return it for eternity," Cornelia explained. Cedric sighed in relief. The end of the staircase became visible. A heavy metal door blocked the entrance to the spell room.

"Push the door open while I recite the magic formula!" Cornelia told Cedric. The formula sounded like the loud croaking of a frog, but no one doubted that Cornelia had pronounced some incomprehensible magic words. Cedric thought that the door also felt hot to the touch. In fact, it seemed hotter than the banister. An amazing scene became visible in front of them. A large cauldron was attached to the ceiling. A group of tiny devils was dancing wildly around it. The agile devils had horns, long tails, and crimson faces. Cornelia pronounced:

"Spires of fire
satisfy my desire!"

Then, she exhaled a red flame. In an instant, the small fire under the cauldron grew with a loud explosion. The flames enveloped the cauldron reaching the ceiling. The cauldron turned a shade of burgundy and a thick, purple liquid began to bubble inside of it. The devils screamed with delight, dancing in the flames. The room was filled with smoke and sparks. The heat became unbearable. The three humans stared at the satanic scene, petrified. They leaned against the wall, keeping away from the fire as much as possible. However, small fragments of hot coals flew in their direction, charring fibers in their clothes. Cornelia circled the cauldron a few times, croaking loudly and, occasionally, exhaling a little flame that seemed to boost the fire. Her orange eyes flashed through the smoke like a lighthouse in the fog. With their clawed hands, the devils grabbed the three humans forcing them to join their wild dance. They filled the room with horrible howls, screeches, and cries. Rebecca, David, and Cedric circled the cauldron with the devils, screaming in terror. Cornelia's high-pitched laughter, intermingled with deep croaks, supplied an interesting counterpoint effect.

"Time to start!" suddenly she said. The devils disappeared inside the cauldron. The humans tried to catch their breath, overwhelmed by the heat and the smoke. Their clothes had turned into charred rags. Their faces were black with soot.

"Open the cabinet on the right side of the window and find a jar filled with juniper powder!" Cornelia addressed Cedric imperatively. Cedric searched the cabinet.

"Juniper powder," he read on one of the labels.

"It's not just juniper powder. I mixed it with the dehydrated skin of a dragon's tail."

"Dragons don't exist!" Rebecca objected.

"Shush, young lady!" Cornelia exhaled a green breath that carved the figure of a dragon into one of the walls.

"You can look inside the cabinet on the left side of the window and find a jar filled with pterodactyl blood!" she told David.

"And you, big mouth, look everywhere and find a jar full of mammoth tusk powder and another one filled with vampire nails!" she told Rebecca.

"I thought vampires were fictional," said Rebecca.

"I suggest that you stop questioning my ingredients, unless you want to end up as 'Rebecca's Powder' in one of those jars," Cornelia said, staring at her angrily. Her eyes turned deep crimson red.

The three humans obeyed meekly, producing the requested items.

"Now I want you to add two pinches of juniper powder, a handful of mammoth tusk powder, one pinch of vampire nails, and a cup of pterodactyl blood into the cauldron." They followed her orders and, after each addition, the bubbly potion sent purple sparks in all directions. Some of the sparks burned a few hairs on Cedric's head.

"Move back! I have to pronounce the magic words," Cornelia thundered, standing in the center of the tower.

The three humans leaned against the wall. Cornelia's slimy skin shone brightly under the moonlight. The flames extending towards the ceiling continued to rage furiously. Cornelia closed her eyelids, revealing only a sliver of her bulbous eyes. She was about to pronounce the spell when, suddenly, the ghost of Lady Rosabel appeared in the room. Like a zombie, she took uncertain steps around the cauldron. Her eyes were filled with tears. Her moans echoed inside the tower.

"Lady Rosabel, why are you in my spell tower?" Cornelia asked with a raspy voice. The ghost ignored her question and walked in the direction of the three humans. She stared at them for some time. Finally, she pleaded, "Please, help me! Osmar cursed me."

"Where's Osmar?" Cedric asked.

"He's in the cauldron. Please, help me!" she repeated.

Right at that moment someone knocked at the door. Cornelia was visibly annoyed.

"Who's there?" she thundered.

The door screeched as it opened, revealing the tall, dark figure of Holbrook.

"I'm sorry, but a man and an elf are here to see you, Lady Cornelia," said the butler.

"An elf? What kind of crazy, fearless elf would knock at my door? Does this elf know who I am?"

"It's an elf woman. They are friends of Lodema the witch," Holbrook added.

"Let them in!" Cornelia croaked. She didn't like to have her spells interrupted. Paul and Esther boldly stepped into the tower, like two secret agents on a dangerous mission.

"Paul!" Rebecca screamed, as she saw her brother. She forgot about the flames, the ghost, and the witch, springing in the direction of the door. She hugged both Paul and Esther, crying. David and Cedric joined them, warmly shaking hands.

"Weren't you supposed to be on your honeymoon? What are you doing here?" Rebecca asked.

"The elves released by Cornelia came running into the Clear Creek area, next to the wood, chased by some evil spirits. Jarman helped them. They told us that you were here," Esther explained.

"Are we in some kind of hell?" Paul asked, suddenly taking in the fiery scene in front of him.

"You won't believe what's happening here!" Cedric said. The ghost of Lady Rosabel walked in their direction. She seemed to shake slightly.

"Help me!" she whispered, staring at the group. The pallor of her hands contrasted sharply with the dark circles around her eyes.

"Who is she?" Esther was taken aback.

"The restless ghost of Lady Rosabel. Osmar the sorcerer imprisoned her in his castle, where she died." Cedric explained.

"How can we help you if you're already dead?" Paul asked Lady Rosabel.

"You have to enter the cauldron and step into the past. You must stop Osmar before I die. Otherwise, I'll be a cursed ghost forever."

"Enter the cauldron?" Paul asked, staring at the thick, bubbly potion that leaked down the sides of the big pot, surrounded by tall raging flames.

"I have no magic powers. Esther has limited powers, as compared to a sorcerer. How could we possibly outdo Osmar?" he added.

"I'll help you!" Cornelia croaked from the opposite side of the tower.

"That should make Lodema very happy!" Cedric said.

"Esther and I will go into the cauldron together," said Paul.

"That's a terrible idea! You'll risk your life to help a ghost!" Rebecca screamed.

"We have to do it!" Esther interjected. She and Paul were daredevils. They liked taking risks and they relished the lure of the unknown.

"Please hurry! I'd like to continue with my spell," said Cornelia.

"Aren't they going to boil to death?" asked Rebecca.

"No. I'll make sure that the hot potion won't harm them," said Cornelia. She exhaled a large breath of air in the direction of the fire, under the cauldron. The flames opened up.

"Now get in!" Cornelia ordered. Paul interlocked his fingers allowing Esther to step on top of his hands. She grasped the top of the tall cauldron and pushed herself upwards. The leaking potion was slimy and she slipped down. Paul gave her a push while she grasped the top of the cauldron again. This time, she dove into the cauldron. Rebecca screamed. A few devils popped their heads out of the cauldron.

"Let them in! Don't bother them!" Cornelia ordered. The devils disappeared with a shriek.

"Your turn!" Cornelia said to Paul.

"No! Please, don't go!" Rebecca screamed. Paul hugged his sister.

"Cornelia will help us. We'll be fine!" he reassured her.

"Can Cedric help me step into the cauldron?" he asked Cornelia.

"Sure, but he can't go in with you."

Cedric interlocked his fingers and allowed Paul to step on the back of his hands. Paul leaped and dove into the cauldron like a dolphin into a pool. The potion continued to bubble menacingly. The flames closed in, around the cauldron. Cedric, David, and Rebecca stared at the hellish scene, speechless. Lady Rosabel levitated slightly and floated above the cauldron, moaning. Then, she also disappeared inside of it. The frog had a satisfied expression on her face. Her eyes turned light ochre and gazed at the cauldron with a new softness. She had the kind expression of someone who was about to do a good deed.

Paul hit the ground with a heavy thud, landing a few feet away from Esther. She was sitting on the floor, rubbing one of her arms, still sore from her fall.

"Where are we?" she asked.

"Apparently in the kitchen. If you look out of the window, you can see that we are in a castle."

"It's a large castle, with many turrets connected by bridges," said Esther.

"The kitchen is also very big," said Paul.

"There's an eerie atmosphere in this kitchen," she added, staring at the large brick oven, in which a bright fire was roasting six partridges. Gradually, the couple became aware of a soft moan. Paul and Esther turned their heads and saw Lady Rosabel at the kitchen table. She didn't have the dark circles around her eyes.

"Lady Rosabel!" they exclaimed.

The young woman was perplexed.

"Are you Osmar's friends?" she asked, without recognizing them.

"No. We're here to help you," Esther replied.

"How did you come in?"

"Magic," said Esther.

"That explains it because I'm trapped in here. No one can get in or get out," the young woman said crying.

"What exactly happened to you?" Paul asked her.

"Six months ago, I was about to get married to a lord in my father's kingdom…"

"You're a princess!" Esther remarked.

"A very sad princess. Osmar trapped me in his castle. My family doesn't know that I'm here," Lady Rosabel explained.

"You don't look like a princess. You're wearing rags," Paul interjected.

"We'll release you from this castle," Esther said, while her hair bounced lightly revealing her pointed ears.

"You're elves! You have magic powers!" Lady Rosabel said, gasping.

"I'm an elf. My husband is a human. I have limited powers. Nevertheless, we'll help you," Esther repeated optimistically.

"Are you sure there's no way out of this castle?" Paul asked.

"All the windows are barred and the doors are locked," Lady Rosabel replied. She started sobbing, with her head leaning on the table.

The smell of the roasting partridges attracted Paul's attention. He slowly approached the oven. Suddenly, the flames began to curl into a funnel-shaped spiral over the burning logs. Paul moved closer to the oven and heard a familiar, raspy voice, "Don't waste your time trying to find a way out of the castle."

"It's you! Cornelia!" Paul exclaimed.

"I told you I was going to help you!"

"What are we supposed to do?"

"Wait for Osmar's return! I'll guide you!"

Paul conveyed Cornelia's instructions to his wife, while Lady Rosabel continued to sob. Suddenly, the walls began to shake.

"He's back!" Lady Rosabel cried. "Every time he returns, a small earthquake shakes the entire castle," she explained. "Quick! In the pantry! He'll be here in a moment." Lady Rosabel opened the door of the pantry, pushing the couple inside. Esther and her husband tripped and fell over a large sack of flour. They cleaned the flour off their faces. Paul stared at the sausages hanging on a wall.

"We can watch what happens in the kitchen by looking through that metal grating up there," Esther whispered, drawing Paul's attention away from the sausages. They climbed a ladder that was inside the pantry and looked through the metal bars. Osmar appeared in the kitchen. He was tall and thin. He was wearing a long coat of black brocade with purple embroidery. His cold eyes looked like the eyes of a cat in the night. Lady Rosabel got up from her chair and moved away from him.

"Why can't you greet me with a smile?" he asked. She stared at him, crying.

"Quiet!" he yelled, pushing a few dishes off the kitchen table. She gasped. The loud noise of the cracking dishes was followed by silence. Osmar stood in front of her menacingly. She seemed to be petrified with fear. Gradually, Lady Rosabel's features hardened and her eyes acquired a cutting expression of defiance. She remembered that she was a princess and that she had been taught to give commands.

"Let me go!" she said matter-of-factly.

"I own you!" said Osmar.

"You may own my body, but not my heart."

"I don't need your heart!"

"To have a woman without her heart is to have nothing!" she said boldly.

"In time, I'll own your heart also."

"Never! My heart belongs to another man," she said. Osmar turned into a cyclone of fury.

"If you want to leave my castle, you're free to go!" he said. With a hand gesture, he made the window disappear, and pushed Lady Rosabel out of the tower. While falling, she felt the strong tendrils of a vine plant tighten around her arms and legs, holding her upside down. The plant covered the entire wall of the tower, extending its coils in all directions. Osmar leaped out of the window and gracefully landed in front of the castle.

"Bring her down!" he ordered. The plant slowly lowered Lady Rosabel's body.

"Stop right there!" Osmar said, when she was about 15 feet above the ground.

Paul and Esther left the pantry and approached the oven.

"Cornelia, what should we do?" they asked.

"Jump out of the window!"

They hesitated for a few seconds.

"Let's go!" he said. They closed their eyes and jumped. As they were falling, the tendrils of the vine plant wrapped around Esther, suspending her in mid-air, ten feet above Lady Rosabel. Paul landed on the ground without getting hurt.

"Who are you? How do you dare enter my property?" said Osmar.

"We're friends of Lady Rosabel," Paul answered.

"Nosy intruders!"

By kicking, pulling, and twisting, Esther managed to release her upper body. She was still suspended upside down, with her ankles held by the vine. The plant began to swing back and forth. She screamed. Paul began to climb the tower. The plant extended a couple of coils in his direction, but Paul quickly extracted his magic Swiss army knife from his pocket. It was a gift, given to him by Haralda the witch, in exchange for a couple of porcelain table lamps.

Business always pays! Paul thought. The blade cut through the curled stems without any effort. Paul continued to climb the steep tower wall, stepping on the uneven bricks. Finally, he reached Esther and severed the tendrils holding her ankles. They both leaped and landed safely on the ground.

"In the pond!" Osmar yelled. A magic wind swept the couple into a pond, at the center of his garden. They resurfaced for a couple of seconds. Esther took a large breath of air and went underwater again. Paul followed her. Her elf instinct had been attracted by the presence of gold. She knew that there was a buried treasure, somewhere in the pond. She resurfaced to catch another breath of air, followed by her husband.

"What are you doing? We have to help Lady Rosabel!" he said.

"If my instinct is right, Osmar hid a stolen treasure right below us," she said.

"Another stolen treasure? Do these sorcerers spend their entire life stealing and hiding treasures?"

"Yes, the evil ones usually do."

"I'll take care of Osmar while you find the treasure!" a large frog standing near the pond spoke with Cornelia's voice. The frog hopped away.

"Let's go back in!" Esther said. She began to test the bottom of the pond with her sensitive hands, occasionally resurfacing to breathe. Finally, she stopped and her hands started to shake. She looked at Paul and smiled. They both resurfaced.

"We need a sharp tool. The knife won't work," said Paul.

"It's a magic knife! Try it!" she said. They went underwater and Paul pointed the knife in the precise spot indicated by his wife. The blade cut through the rock without any effort. They found an old chest and brought it out of the water. Paul cut the lock and opened it. The chest was filled with five sparkling green diamonds. Like a happy elf next to a very valuable treasure, Esther began to dance, pirouetting and kicking her feet up in the air. Paul was astounded.

"What are these?" he asked.

"They are magic diamonds that belong to Jarman. If we return this treasure to him, he'll give us a large reward in gold coins!" she said. They hid the chest under a large bush. Then, they walked to the front of the castle to check how Cornelia was handling Lady Rosabel's rescue. A very dramatic scene took shape in front of their eyes. Osmar was holding Lady Rosabel by her hair.

"Let me go," she screamed.

"No, you'll stay with me forever."

"You're the most wicked creature in the world!"

"That's right! I'm also the most powerful one!" he said. A loud, sudden croak echoed in the air.

"You're wrong! I can be more evil and more powerful than you!" Cornelia's eyes burned like red coals. She exhaled a large flame from her mouth, which surrounded Osmar. He began to burn and the vine plant began to shrivel. The flame slowly made his body vanish. Finally, only his eyes were visible, two desperate eyes filled with anger, the eyes of a dying evil sorcerer. His eyes also disappeared, as the plant fell off the wall, completely wilted. A tall, beautiful woman stood next to Lady Rosabel. It was Lodema the witch.

"You succeeded in doing something very good! You reversed Lady Rosabel's curse and the curse on David's bakery, by destroying Osmar. You're free from my enchantment. You're no longer a frog or an ugly and warty witch. Now your outer appearance reflects your new good disposition. Keep up the good work if you don't want me to turn you into an amphibian again!" Lodema said and vanished.

"I'm not sure I like my new identity. I liked my green complexion and my wiry hair!" Cornelia complained, as she touched her long smooth hair.

"You have to see yourself in a mirror. You really look amazing!" Paul said.

Esther produced a mirror, which she always carried in her pocket. Cornelia stared at her new image. Her eyes were a shade of gold, with the unmistakable metallic reflection that was typical of witches. Her face was not young, but not old. It was the beautiful face of a mature woman who hadn't started to age.

"What drove you to confront Osmar?" Paul asked.

"Osmar challenged me! He couldn't be more evil and more powerful than me!" she said proudly.

"Osmar was a fool. No one can challenge a witch!" said Esther.

"I thought that you turned into a good witch," said Paul.

"Possibly…but I'm not sure I like myself yet," she said, with a sinister light in her eyes. Paul shook his head, uncomprehendingly.

"Lady Rosabel, close your eyes and count to ten! When you reopen your eyes, you'll be in front of your father's castle," Cornelia told the princess, who was no longer wearing rags. Lady Rosabel hugged Paul and Esther. Then, she followed Cornelia's instructions, vanishing.

"Now, let's go get the treasure!" said Paul.

The couple walked back to the pond and showed the chest to Cornelia.

"It belongs to Jarman. It was stolen from him several years ago," Esther told her.

"An excellent find! It will be useful to you," Cornelia said.

"How do we leave the past and return to the present?" Paul asked.

"Hold on to the chest and let's leap together at the end of my chant." She sang some incomprehensible words, while her eyes turned a dark bronze color. They leaped out of the cauldron and landed on the floor of the spell room. They were greeted by David, Rebecca, Cedric, and Holbrook.

"Lady Cornelia, you look wonderful! I'm so glad you regained human features!" said the butler.

"Holbrook, don't count on my new features. I may decide to change them from time to time! However, I will not defy Lodema because I don't want to be turned into another frog."

"Yes, that's very inconvenient," said Holbrook.

Paul and Esther recounted all the events that had occurred and revealed the contents of the chest they had found.

"Now, are you going to continue your honeymoon?" Rebecca asked her sister.

"So far, we've been enjoying our honeymoon!" Esther said. "Next, we're going to return the chest. Jarman will give us a large reward, which we can add to our gold pots. Paul also has a gold pot!" she said.

"You're really made for each other! Time to go back to my bakery!" David said.

"Take good care of my shop!" Paul told Cedric, beginning to go down the stairs with Esther.

"Be careful!" Rebecca said from the top of the staircase, with a worried expression on her face.

5

The Green Diamonds

The sun had just started to rise when Paul and Esther set out on their journey to Jarman's house. They reached the creek and followed the path next to it, at a very relaxed pace. The gentle sound of the water and the cool breeze of the morning had a soothing effect on them, after their dreadful experience in Cornelia's spell room. Paul was carrying the chest of green diamonds and admiring its elegant carvings. It was an antique wood chest, made of polished elm, with rosewood inserts. He placed it on the ground and opened it to inspect its inner condition.

"I'll ask Jarman if I can keep this chest. I know I can sell it easily in my shop. I'm sure that many women would like to have it as a jewelry box," he said. Esther looked at the chest distractedly and changed the subject.

"Paul, after the frantic adventures we've had recently, I wish we could enjoy a quiet candlelight dinner in a restaurant," she said. To their amazement, one of the green diamonds inside the chest shone brightly, attracting their attention. As they stared at the diamond, they were enveloped by a green halo that became a thick fog. When they were finally able to see their surroundings again, they realized that they were no longer on the path that bordered the wood, next to the creek. Instead, they were sitting at an outdoor table, in a restaurant overlooking the ocean. They were no longer wearing the clothes that had been torn by the devils and darkened by the smoke in Cornelia's spell room. Paul was wearing a Hawaiian shirt and a pair of nice slacks, and Esther had a long summer dress on. The sun was setting on the horizon, and a candle was lit in the middle of their table. Esther and her husband laughed.

"Those diamonds can grant wishes!" he said, at the same time realizing that they no longer had the chest in their possession. Esther became very serious.

"We must have left the chest next to the creek. I wish we had hidden it," she said. Immediately, a green halo enveloped them, gradually turning into a thick fog. When they were finally able to see their surroundings, they realized they were next to the creek again. They were still wearing their new clothes and there was a shovel on the ground.

"This means that we're here only temporarily..." she reasoned.

"...to hide the chest," he added.

"However, we are using our second wish," she said.

They dug a hole next to an oak and proceeded to conceal the chest, covering it with dirt, leaves, and a large rock on top. As soon as their job was completed, the green light surrounded them one more time, taking them back to the restaurant.

"Where do you think we are?" she asked.

"Judging from the music, we're in the Caribbean," said Paul.

"Weren't we headed on a mission to Jarman's house?" Esther asked, with a worried expression.

"First things first!" Paul said. They placed their dinner orders, starting to enjoy their evening together. The waiter brought a broiled lobster in a covered plate for Paul and a seafood salad for Esther. Paul lifted the lid and heard a soft voice coming from his dish:

"Please help me! My life's in danger!"

As he looked closer into the dish, he saw a tiny mermaid lying on one of the halved lobster shells. He immediately covered his dish.

"I don't really want to eat this. I changed my mind," he said, trying to find the waiter. Esther, who had also heard and seen the mermaid, stopped him.

"Her life's in danger! We must help her!"

"What about our beautiful evening together?" he asked.

"We can't pretend we didn't hear her!"

"Why? Have we been enlisted by an undercover organization, dedicated to the rescue of people in distress?" he asked.

"Very funny! Lift the lid and let's find out what her problem is!"

He sighed with resignation and uncovered his plate, at the same time inhaling the delicious smell of lobster that spread over the table.

"I hope you won't mind if I take a few bites of the lobster," he told the mermaid, determined to eat his meal, regardless of the chain of events that surely was going to lead to another wild adventure. Esther picked up the mermaid with two fingers and held her in the palm of her hand, while Paul started eating.

"I'm Esther and this is my husband. We're on our honeymoon," she introduced herself and Paul in a friendly fashion.

"I'm so sorry to intrude, but I'm in desperate need of help," said the mermaid.

"What happened? We can help you," Esther said optimistically. Paul nodded with his head, as he was chewing a large piece of lobster.

"I'm Nila, the daughter of the baker on this island," the mermaid began her account.

Another bakery crisis! Paul thought, digging his fork into the lobster shell.

"A sorcerer kidnapped me, turned me into a mermaid, and sold me to the Lobster King."

"Is he some sort of giant crustacean?" Paul asked, chewing his dinner with gusto.

"No, the Lobster King is an underwater sorcerer who has power over all types of lobsters. He kept me as a caged bird. I had to entertain him with my voice."

"Who is the other sorcerer?" Esther inquired.

"He came into my father's bakery one day and heard me singing. I have a very good voice. That's why he kidnapped me and sold me to the Lobster King."

"How did you end up on my plate?" Paul asked, confused.

"I managed to escape from the cage and swam away from the Lobster King's underwater castle. I was caught in a fisherman's net and brought to this restaurant, where no one has seen me yet, except for the two of you," she explained.

"In other words, you're free!" said Esther.

"Not really. I'm a mermaid, which means that I need to live in seawater or my scales will dry out and I'll die, but if you throw me back into the ocean, either the Lobster King will cage me or some other terrible fate awaits me. There are sharks, barracudas, and other horrible creatures underwater, constantly looking for their prey." Esther gasped in horror. She held the mermaid by the arms and dropped her into her glass of water.

"It's not as good as seawater, but at least your scales will be moist," she said.

The mermaid took a large breath of air and went underwater.

"We need to reverse her spell. We could use one of the magic green diamonds and make another wish!" Paul suggested.

"No, you can't reverse a sorcerer's spell that easily," said Esther.

"Then, we need to find the sorcerer who turned her into a mermaid in order to reverse the spell," said Paul.

The mermaid's head reemerged.

"I'm afraid that we need the help of a witch. Witches know how to handle these situations," said Esther.

"You're not suggesting…"

"Yes! We have to go back to Cornelia's house!" said Esther. The couple decided to proceed with this plan. With sadness, Esther glanced at the peaceful ocean, at the candle in the middle of the table, and at the live band that was filling the night with calypso music.

"I'll make the third wish. We would like to go to Cornelia's house," Paul said. He waited for a few seconds, but nothing happened. "Aren't the green diamonds granting us the wish?" he asked with disappointment. Esther laughed.

"The green diamonds belong to an elf. They can only grant an elf's wish," she explained. "I'll make the third wish."

"Just a minute! I don't want to go to Cornelia's house! I'm sure that we can find a different solution…" Nila tried to stop her.

Esther picked her up with two fingers, ignoring her objections, and quickly repeated the wish. Instantly they were surrounded by a green light that turned into fog. When the fog had dissipated, they found themselves on the porch of Cornelia's house. They knocked at the door and Holbrook's ghostly figure appeared.

"Sorry to be back so soon, but we need Cornelia's help," Paul explained.

The butler led them to a living room with a fireplace.

"Let me call Lady Cornelia and get some sherry," Holbrook said.

"We also need a bowl of water for this mermaid," Esther added, revealing the presence of Nila in the palm of her hand. Before Holbrook returned, Cornelia made a dramatic appearance.

She materialized from the flames of the fireplace, with a loud cackle.

"It's good to see you! What brings you here?" she asked, standing next to the fireplace. Her eyes reflected the light of the fire, turning a shade of red orange. Paul related the events that had recently occurred on the island, while Esther showed the mermaid to the witch. Cornelia burst into laughter. Her loud voice made the chandelier sway back and forth with a wide motion. The logs in the fireplace cracked loudly and the flames produced a sizzling sound.

"This is not a baker's daughter!" Cornelia finally said. Right at that moment, Holbrook returned, holding a large bucket filled with water and a few rose petals, and a tray with three glasses.

"I see that Lady Cornelia is already here," he commented with a robotic tone of voice and a grave expression.

"We won't need that bucket. Smyrna can regain her human features anytime she decides to do so," said Cornelia.

"Smyrna? Her name isn't Nila?" Esther was dumbfounded.

"No. I recognize her face. She's a witch and she turned herself into a mermaid," Cornelia explained.

"Are you sure?" Paul asked.

"I know her and I can recognize her even if she tries to change her appearance. I'm 300 years older than she is," said Cornelia. Esther was very upset. Her candlelight dinner with Paul had been interrupted by a lying witch that pretended to need help. She threw the mermaid into the bucket angrily. The mermaid instantly gained her witch appearance, stepping out of the bucket.

"I really need your help! I just didn't know how to tell you what really happened…" she told Esther, while her purple eyes sparkled like amethysts, producing a slightly hypnotic effect. Esther stepped back, feeling the witch's power with alarm.

"What's the problem?" asked Cornelia.

"What happened to your hair and your face?" Smyrna asked Cornelia, delaying her explanation.

"Lodema decided that I should look beautiful. Isn't she annoying? For five hundred and sixty-years I've been ugly and mean. Now, all of a sudden, I'm supposed to be good and beautiful!"

"Who does she think she is?" Smyrna said, siding with her.

"And if I don't comply with her insane need to be righteous, she'll turn me into a frog!"

"How inconvenient! You can hardly use your magic powers in that state," Smyrna sympathized.

"It's that husband of hers! When they marry humans, they turn into mush and forget what witches are supposed to be like!" Cornelia exclaimed.

The mention of his category stirred Paul from his silence.

"Perhaps Esther and I could find out what Smyrna's predicament is or, possibly, return to our tropical island."

"I have a 20-year-old daughter who has been trapped in the ocean by Zadok, a real underwater sorcerer," said Smyrna.

"Doesn't your daughter have special powers?" asked Paul.

"No, Drusilla was conceived with a human... and she took after her father..."

"Smyrna! How could you? A human?" Cornelia asked, in consternation. Smyrna looked absolutely mortified.

"I met him in the wood...there was a full moon...I don't know how it happened...but I fell in love with him and I lived with him 35 fantastic years until he died," Smyrna confessed in one breath, like a child who has been caught stealing an apple from a private orchard. A tear rolled down her face.

"We'll help you! Tell us more about Drusilla's case!" Esther said.

"Six months ago, Zadok kidnapped Drusilla. He keeps her in a cave of his underwater palace, guarded by a giant octopus. The cave is magically equipped with air, but she can't escape. She can't communicate with me because she has no magic powers. However,

I can feel her emotions and I know she's miserable." Smyrna paused to wipe the tears that were now rolling down in copious amounts.

"Why can't you save her? Aren't you more powerful than Zadok?" asked Paul.

"No, Zadok is the son of a witch. He's as powerful as any witch. He'd recognize me, even if I changed my appearance. I couldn't go into his palace unnoticed."

"Why did you choose us?" Esther asked.

"I chose you and your husband because everyone in Green Wood knows that you're clever, skilled, and fearless. Zadok lives underwater and doesn't know about your existence. You're the perfect couple to undertake this mission, which requires courage and diplomacy," said Smyrna.

"We'll help you," Esther repeated.

"No obstacle can separate us from a new adventure," Paul said with excitement in his voice.

"You'll need Cornelia's support, because she's much older and more experienced than I am," said Smyrna.

Cornelia shifted her gaze sluggishly from one guest to another.

"What makes you think that I'll help? What do I get in return?" Cornelia asked, while her eyes turned an opaque rusty color, devoid of any sparkle. Paul approached her with a warm, friendly smile.

"Cornelia, I'm the owner of the best shop of house furnishings in the county. Not only do I sell all types of furnishings--modern, antique, original, imitation--but I can also satisfy any request in the most efficient and discreet manner. I noticed that you have a beautiful Victorian mahogany table and a spectacular rococo chandelier. I also noticed your Louis XV fireplace mantel, your British walnut cabinet, and your French Napoleonic candelabra. Since you seem to collect antique furniture and decorative pieces of highly exquisite taste, I can be of invaluable help to you. If you assist us in this mission, I'll find any type of furnishing that you desire, at no cost." Cornelia smiled a womanly smile, as she thought for a moment of the many possible additions to her house.

"It's a deal!" she said.

"Why did Zadok kidnap your daughter?" Esther asked Smyrna.

"I don't know."

"We'll find out," said Paul.

"I'm going to give you temporary gills, which will allow you to swim underwater without having to reemerge for air," said Cornelia.

"What about the octopus?" Esther asked.

"I have a special potion that will make the octopus fall asleep. Follow me!" said Cornelia, leading the way to her spell room. Paul followed her, resigned to the idea of entering hell a second time. As they were climbing the spiral staircase of the spell room tower, the image of a skeleton appeared in the center. Smyrna pointed her finger in his direction and enunciated,

Back to the land of the dead
Leave alone a witch that is mad!

She blinked a few times and a purple light surrounded the skeleton, who vanished.

"We don't have time for additional curses," she added. Cornelia agreed, opening the door of her spell room. A small group of devils was jumping up and down in a puddle of potion that had spilled out of the bubbling cauldron. As they jumped, they changed color from sky blue to hot pink, to yellow, green, and back to sky blue. Cornelia snapped her fingers, reducing the length of the flames that surrounded the cauldron. As soon as they saw her, the devils disappeared inside the pot. Paul and Esther stood against the wall coughing, due to the thick smoke. Cornelia opened a cabinet, extracted a vial filled with a clear liquid and gave it to Paul.

"When you're close to the octopus, pour this potion!" she instructed him.

"It's time to go back to the tropical island. Let's stand in a circle." Smyrna said.

She blinked a few times, surrounding the group with a purple light. As the light vanished, they were on the beach of the tropical island.

"Now you have gills. You're ready to go," Cornelia said. Paul and Esther touched their heads behind their ears and smiled. Before entering the water, Esther hesitated.

"How do we find the cave?" she asked.

"Follow the polka dot grouper," Cornelia replied.

"We'll wait on the beach," said Smyrna.

Paul and Esther entered the water. For a while, they swam without a specific direction in mind, testing their ability to go to different depths without having to worry about pressure and lack of oxygen. They began to enjoy themselves, feeling as comfortable as fish. They chased each other along a colorful coral reef, and played hide and seek in the middle of a school of tiny tropical fish. Suddenly, a red grouper with blue polka dots made a few circles around them. They followed the grouper along a course that zigzagged among steep rocks. They sighted the giant octopus. The monster resembled a gigantic open umbrella with tentacles over 20 feet in length. Holding the precious vial, Paul swam towards the octopus, but one of its tentacles grabbed his arm and pushed him away from the cave. The potion spread in the water without touching the octopus. Instead, it came in contact with the grouper, which instantly fell asleep. Another tentacle grabbed Esther by her waist and also pushed her away. Inside the cave, which magically didn't contain any water, Drusilla was unaware of what was happening. She was sitting in a corner, trying to come up with an escape plan. Paul and Esther continued to make multiple attempts to reach the cave. The infuriated octopus began to shake its tentacles violently in all directions, creating underwater waves, which turned to the couple's advantage, as they pushed Paul and Esther toward the cave entrance. The water crashed into the cave, threatening to drown Drusilla. Instinctively, she stood up and with her palms facing the incoming water, she screamed,

"Stop! Be still!
Obey my will!"

The ocean instantly turned very calm and the octopus stopped moving. Drusilla gasped with surprise. She looked at her hands and noticed that her nails were long and curved. She also realized that the long smooth locks of her hair were gently coiling into spirals.

"You're a witch!" Paul said, as he entered the cave with Esther.

Drusilla gasped a second time.

"I didn't know I was a witch," Drusilla mumbled.

"Your mother will be happy," said Paul.

"Do you know my mother?"

"She sent us to save you, but maybe you can get us all out of here now," Esther said.

"It's not so simple. If I leave this cave, the gears of Zadok's mantel clock will stop turning and his daughter will die."

"Does Zadok have a daughter?"

"Yes, but she has no magic powers. She has gills, given to her by her mother who was a witch. Zadok's wife had a fight with another witch who cursed her daughter. The life of Zadok's daughter depends on the turning gears of his mantel clock. The clock works only if Zadok keeps a witch or the daughter of a witch captive in his underwater palace. Zadok kidnapped me to keep his daughter alive. Like everyone else, he thought that I had no powers and that I wouldn't be able to escape."

"Surely, since you're a witch, you should be able to reverse the curse now," said Esther.

"My mother never trained me because she assumed that I was a regular human. I don't know the first thing about curses and magic potions and magic spells. I don't know any magic formulas. I never learned anything about magic herbs and…." Drusilla started crying.

"Just our luck: a witch with no magic knowledge!" said Paul.

"Can't you just improvise as you did when you calmed the octopus and the ocean?" Esther insisted.

"I was about to drown then…my reaction was instinctive. Now I really wouldn't know what to do to save Zadok's daughter."

"The best thing that we can do is to take the mantel clock to Cornelia. Perhaps she may be able to destroy its cursing power," Paul told Esther.

The couple left the cave, swimming through the dangling tentacles of the octopus. They searched through the thick vegetation until they found a rock with a golden door. It was the main entrance to the underwater castle and it was locked. As they were trying to decide how to enter the castle, another grouper with blue polka dots made a couple of circles around them.

"Look! Cornelia sent us another grouper!" said Esther.

"Let's follow it!"

The grouper led them to the golden roof of the castle and circled the chimney a couple of times. Paul and Esther peeked into the opening of the chimney, but couldn't see anything.

"We have to play Santa Claus!" Paul commented.

"Judging from the lack of smoke, there's no fire at the bottom," said Esther. She inserted her legs into the opening and realized that the chimney, just like the cave, contained no water. They landed in the fireplace with a loud bang.

"What are you doing here?" The voice of a young woman drew their attention.

"Who are you?" Esther asked.

"I'm Rosalin, Zadok's daughter, the lady of the castle. You must be intruders!" she said with haughtiness.

"No, we're friends. We're actually here to save your life," said Paul.

"Why? Am I in danger?"

"Yes," he replied, taking the mantel clock.

"Don't touch that clock or my father will be very angry!" said Rosalin.

"We don't have time for a lengthy explanation, but your father is keeping a young woman captive in the cave and your life is in danger," said Esther.

"My father would never hold anyone captive," Rosalin said.

"Follow us to the cave. We'll show you," said Esther.

"I'm taking the clock. It's for your protection," said Paul.

They quickly walked towards the entrance, followed by Rosalin, and left the castle. They swam towards the cave, where they found Drusilla eagerly waiting for them.

"Why is the octopus asleep?" Rosalin inquired.

No one answered her question.

"Have you ever heard of Cornelia the witch?" Esther asked her.

"I'm afraid not."

"Have you heard of Smyrna the witch?" Esther asked.

"No, I don't know much about witches. My parents didn't teach me anything about witchcraft because I have no magic powers. My mother was a witch and my father is a sorcerer, but most of my relatives on my father's side of the family are humans," she explained.

Paul shook his head. Not only was he caught in another situation that involved magic, which he strongly disliked, but he also had to deal with an untrained witch and the daughter of two magic parents who claimed to have no special powers. Additionally, out of the corner of his eye, he noticed that the octopus was waking up and starting to flex its tentacles outside the cave. He sat down, mulling over the complicated situation.

"Who are you? Why are you here? Why did you take the mantel clock? And who is the woman in the cave?" Rosalin asked.

"This is Drusilla, the daughter of Smyrna the witch," Esther began to share all the facts with Rosalin.

"I'm so sorry" Rosalin said crying, when she heard the reason for Drusilla's captivity.

"We'll take the clock to Cornelia so that she can reverse the curse," said Esther.

"The problem is that the octopus woke up and won't allow us to leave the cave," said Paul.

"There is a hidden passage that leads from the cave into the castle," said Rosalin. She knocked on the wall behind them and a secret door opened. Rosalin led the way into the castle through a long hallway and showed Esther and her husband an unguarded exit door. Paul and Esther left and followed the grouper that was waiting for them outside the castle. They reached the beach where the two witches were sitting in front of a small fire. There were no burning logs under the fire. Paul ignored this absurd detail, having become accustomed to repeated magic occurrences that defied logic. He disclosed the results of the rescue mission and produced the ticking mantel clock.

"You're asking too much from me: now I have to save two people instead of one!" said Cornelia.

Smyrna was crying tears of joy, having heard that her daughter had magic powers.

"I could have trained her and she'd have been able to save her own life," she kept repeating.

"Stop blaming yourself Smyrna! I'll save her, but you owe me one!" said Cornelia.

Cornelia took the clock and placed it on the bonfire. Everyone screamed. The flames engulfed the clock, which burned for a few minutes, and then exploded.

"Oh my gosh, you killed Rosalin!" Esther exclaimed.

"You are a bunch of fools! How could you possibly believe that the life of a sorcerer's daughter, who is also a witch's daughter, could depend on the ticking of a mantel clock?" said Cornelia.

"Then why is Zadok keeping Drusilla captive, if his daughter isn't in danger?" Paul asked.

"I'm not sure," said Cornelia.

"Drusilla is definitely stuck in the cave because she has no gills and we cannot give her gills from here," said Smyrna.

Then, we'll go to the cave!" said Cornelia.

Smyrna wiped her tears and started spinning like a small tornado. Cornelia followed her example. Gradually, the two witches became shorter and shorter. Finally, they stopped their movement and appeared to have turned into dolphins. They dragged their bodies to the water, with some difficulty. Paul and Esther followed the witches, swimming towards Zadok's castle. They reached the giant octopus, but before it could grab anyone with its tentacles, Cornelia exhaled some bubbles of air that deprived the monster of its liveliness. The octopus floated like a jellyfish and eventually left. They entered the cave. Paul and Esther opened the secret door that led into the castle. Rosalin and Drusilla were eagerly waiting for them. Cornelia and Smyrna had regained their normal appearance.

"What did you do with the mantel clock?" asked Rosalin.

"Don't worry. You're not in danger. Your father made up the story of the clock to keep Drusilla from escaping," said Esther.

"I need to speak to your father," Cornelia told Rosalin with authority.

Obediently, Rosalin showed her the way to Zadok's spell tower. The sorcerer was at his desk, decoding some strange characters in a large book.

"Hello Zadok!" Cornelia greeted him, entering the room.

Zadok raised his head.

"Cornelia, what a surprise! You look wonderful!" he said, with manly appreciation for her beautiful new features. For a moment, her eyes sparkled with an intense orange light. She paused for a few seconds, staring at him. He hadn't lost his youthful appearance, in spite of his advanced age.

"The years didn't change you," she said.

"Many years passed. Many things happened," he said.

"I know. I know everything. I heard that your wife Leandra died and that you have a daughter."

"Yes. Why are you interested in my life? Why are you here?"

"I've been under one of Lodema's spells for a long time and I'm no longer the mean witch that you used to know. I'm here to save a young woman's life."

"Are you meddling with my magic?" Zadok asked with annoyance.

"Why are you keeping Drusilla captive?" Cornelia asked, ignoring his irritation.

"You know I'm a good sorcerer. I'm not keeping her here without a good reason," he replied.

"What's the reason? Is her presence protecting your powers or guaranteeing your daughter's wellbeing in some mysterious way?"

"I've been summoned to a Witch Council meeting, in Hildreth's castle. As you know, Hildreth is the oldest living witch on earth. She wants Drusilla to discover her extraordinary magic powers naturally.

"Wasn't her mother invited to the meeting?"

"No, Hildreth is afraid that her mother may interfere, even if with good intentions."

"Drusilla accidentally discovered her magic powers. Is she free to go now?" Cornelia asked.

"No, not until she figures out how to escape from this castle. Only then, she'll rightfully be a witch," Zadok explained.

"In other words, the kidnapping, the story of the mantel clock, and the giant octopus were all deceiving tricks."

"They were schemes to create the appropriate conditions, in which Drusilla could discover her superior identity."

"You're mad! You shouldn't have gone along with this plan. If it hadn't been for Smyrna, that girl would have been sitting in your cave, crying, for the rest of her life!" Cornelia objected.

"I had no choice. I couldn't oppose the Witch Council members. They're very powerful and dangerous witches. However, I was sure that, sooner or later, Smyrna would have found her way to her daughter. A mother's love knows no limits."

"You're clever, Zadok!"

"The Council doesn't want any interference in this matter. No one, including myself, is supposed to take any action that may affect the natural course of things. Therefore, make sure you don't tell Smyrna, Drusilla or anyone else about the plan," said Zadok.

"Don't worry, I won't disclose this information. However, I may be able to help Drusilla indirectly."

"You're wonderful, Cornelia! I can't recognize you. Since when do you help others?"

"Since never…I'm still the same mean, old witch, Zadok! Lodema wanted me to change and I have to admit that she did succeed in some way, but I'm not happy about it.

Besides, if I help Drusilla, I'll gain free antique furniture for my house," she added. Zadok laughed.

Cornelia left Zadok's spell room and joined the rest of the group.

"What did he say?" Smyrna asked.

"Is he freeing Drusilla?" Rosalin asked.

"No. He cannot free Drusilla and there's nothing we can do to help her."

"Nothing?" Smyrna repeated.

"No. We have to leave the castle immediately and Drusilla has to stay in the cave," said Cornelia.

"For how long?" Smyrna asked.

"I don't know."

"I'll give her gills to allow her to escape," Smyrna said.

"If you do, you'll be in serious trouble," said Cornelia.

Everyone gasped. Drusilla hugged her mother.

"Why is Zadok keeping her captive?" asked Paul. Cornelia didn't reply.

"He must have a very good reason. My father isn't evil," said Rosalin.

"Drusilla has to stay in the cave and we have to leave," said Cornelia.

They walked in the direction of the cave entrance as if they were going to bury a dead person. Drusilla hugged her mother one last time and sat in a corner, accepting her fate passively.

"I didn't bear this daughter to keep her in a prison, waiting to die. I'm not leaving until she leaves," said Smyrna.

"You must leave with us or you'll be in danger," said Cornelia.

"Did Zadok say he'd hurt my mother?" Drusilla asked, awakening from her state of stupor.

"As a matter of fact, he said that anyone who interfered with his secret plan would be in danger," Cornelia replied. She grabbed Smyrna's arm and tried to pull her out of the cave. Smyrna freed her arm.

"I'm not leaving and I'll die if I have to. I'm not leaving Drusilla in the cave alone," she said.

"It's time to go," said Cornelia. She left the cave, followed by Paul and Esther.

"Please, go Smyrna! I'll stay with Drusilla." said Rosalin.

"My mother won't be harmed!" Drusilla's voice resounded loudly inside the cave. It was a dark voice that caused a series of ripples in the ocean. She pointed at the secret door that led into the castle, making it vanish. Then she crossed the hallway and climbed the stairs with the light step of a ferocious feline, ready to pounce on its prey. She entered Zadok's spell room like a fury and blew air with her mouth, creating a ripping wind that circled inside the spell tower. It tore books, cracked lamps, pictures, and bookshelves. It pushed Zadok against a wall. The doors of a black cabinet, containing jars filled with spell ingredients, exploded. With the power of her eyes, Drusilla lifted the desk and the chair and let them drop heavily on the floor, destroying them.

"Do you really think that I'll sit in your cave and watch my mother leave?" she told Zadok, with a deep voice that shook the tower walls.

He stared at her quietly.

"I'm leaving and you will not hurt my mother!" Drusilla confronted him angrily. She touched one of the papers that were flying in the chaos she had caused in the tower. It caught on fire and quickly spread the flames.

"I'll destroy your tower and your castle!" The walls of the spell tower started to collapse and water began to pour into the room.

"Stop!" Zadok cried, raising his arm and quickly repairing the damage.

Drusilla became angrier.

She pointed her finger at the wall and a large waterfall inundated the room. Then, she quickly recited,

You shall crawl, very small,
Through the pieces of your wall!

Zadok shrank instantly, becoming a worm. Drusilla laughed. The worm produced a few sparks and instantly grew in size becoming a lion, while the wall was intact again. Drusilla blew some air into her hand making a spear materialize. She stabbed the lion. The sorcerer regained his human form, stepping out of the lion's skin. He had a sword in his hand and approached the young witch. Smyrna and Rosalin, who had been watching the magic confrontation, screamed. Smyrna stepped forward, thrusting her body between Zadok and her daughter. Zadok's sword cracked.

"It's time to go!" said Smyrna.

"I know," said Drusilla. She blinked and made the entire castle shake violently. A river of water began to flow in. Drusilla spun like a top, at the same time pointing her fingers at Smyrna. They turned into swordfish and swam out of the collapsing castle. Rosalin, who had magic gills, and Zadok, who had turned himself into a bluefin tuna, followed them. Drusilla and Smyrna reached the beach where Paul, Esther, and Cornelia were drying themselves around the fire. The flames turned very bright, signaling the arrival of the witches. Esther looked in the shallow water and saw the two large swordfish approaching.

"They're here!" she said.

Drusilla was the first to emerge, followed by her mother.

"You escaped! You're free!" said Esther, hugging them.

"How did you do it?" Paul asked.

"I destroyed the castle!" Drusilla said laughing.

"What a mean witch!" said Cornelia.

"I still don't know how I did it, but it was so easy!"

"You have terrific powers!" said Smyrna.

"Congratulations!" Zadok said, appearing in front of them with Rosalin.

"You were wonderful!" said Rosalin.

"Why are you congratulating me? Aren't you mad that I destroyed your castle?" Drusilla asked.

Finally, Zadok explained the entire story, starting from the Witch Council meeting, organized by Hildreth.

"I'm so sorry I had to keep Drusilla as a prisoner in my castle," he said.

"We'll rebuild the castle for you," said Smyrna.

"No, I was getting tired of living underwater. It's time that we move on land. Rosalin needs to learn about the outside world." said Zadok.

Paul and Esther asked Cornelia to remove their gills. They didn't want to be involved in another underwater adventure in the future.

"We're going back to our candlelight dinner," said Esther.

"Thank you for your help, Cornelia. Please don't hesitate to visit my shop," said Paul, before leaving.

The couple walked back to the restaurant. After dinner, Esther suggested:

"We have two wishes left. Let's go to Spain!"

He smiled and agreed. Esther held her husband's hand and said, "I wish to go to Spain!" In an instant they vanished together, surrounded by the green fog. They materialized in front of a Moorish-style building, in Granada.

6

The Moorish Princess

Disappearing from one place and reappearing in a completely different part of the world within a few seconds had a slightly bewildering effect. Paul felt slightly confused as he materialized in front of a large Moorish construction, set against a background of low hills covered with olive trees. He inhaled the intense sweet fragrance, spread by the garden that surrounded the building. The afternoon air was warm and soothing on his face. The deafening sound of the crickets also seemed comfortable. The crickets, the flowers, the solid brick construction instilled a sense of reality into his life. He looked at Esther, who also seemed very real to him, while she was admiring the elaborate lacework carved in the arches of the portico.

"What a beautiful building!" Esther remarked.

"Moorish architecture," said Paul.

"I wouldn't mind living here," she said.

"Yes. I can't imagine meeting any witches or sorcerers or evil goblins here. This place is peaceful and yet majestic."

They walked around the building at a leisurely pace, observing its octagonal tower, its decorated doors, its elaborate windows, and the intricate designs painted on its walls. As they approached the large rectangular fountain in the back of the house, Paul noticed a woman sitting on one of its sides. She was wearing a dark green dress that covered her entire body and a light green veil that covered her head, leaving only her eyes visible. She stared at Paul and Esther insistently.

"Who is she?" Esther whispered.

"She doesn't seem to be a mermaid, which is comforting. She doesn't look like a witch either, although I can't always recognize a witch with certainty," said Paul facetiously. The woman made a hand gesture to greet them. Paul and Esther smiled and moved closer to her. Her black eyes were very attractive and had a commanding quality.

"Are you tourists?" she asked them.

"Yes, we're on our honeymoon," Esther replied.

"How wonderful! Congratulations!"

"Are you a tourist?" Paul asked her.

"No, this is my house. I used to live here, over 500 years ago. I'm the Sultan's daughter."

Paul and Esther wondered if they should have bowed respectfully, but remained frozen with surprise.

"Are you a ghost?" Paul asked with a worried undertone in his voice. He feared that this encounter was going to lead to another rescue mission.

"No, I'm not a ghost. My name is Malika. I was born in this house and I lived here until our Grand Vizier poisoned my entire family, except for my grandmother and me. I was able to be transported into your time period thanks to this ring," she said, showing the unusual jewel on her finger. It was a golden ring with four gems.

"Is this a magic ring?" Paul asked redundantly.

"Yes. Each gem has a special power. When I rub a specific gem, I can benefit from its power. The topaz lets me become invisible, the ruby allows me to go through objects, the sapphire makes me heal, and the emerald allows me to travel in time," she explained.

"That's a fantastic ring! You're basically immortal if you wear it," said Esther.

"My grandmother gave it to me and made me promise never to take it off my finger. She has magic powers. However, I'm not immortal. The gems have a limited effect. I can only heal minor ailments. My ability to become invisible and go through objects does not affect my mortality. I'm only allowed to time travel three times in my entire life and I have already used two of them. First, I tried to save my parents by going to a time that preceded their death. Ahmed, the Grand Vizier, caught me and locked me in a tower. Then, I rubbed the emerald very hard trying to travel to the future, in order to free myself. I was transported straight to your era."

"Did you just get here?" Paul asked, with the challenging tone of a disbeliever.

"I've been here for a couple of hours and I'm amazed to see that this building is in such a dilapidated state."

A sudden breeze blew the veil off her head, revealing her young features and her long black, curly hair. She immediately covered her head and face, apologizing to the couple.

"This building looks very beautiful to me," said Esther.

"That's because you don't know how it looked 500 years ago. It had more towers and the wall decorations were brighter. The garden was larger, but the fountain looks the same. That's why I've been sitting here."

"You'll have to resign yourself to living in our time. We have beautiful houses too. You may find life in our age interesting," said Paul. Malika shrieked at the thought of living in the modern time.

"You don't understand, I'm the sultan's daughter! How could you possibly expect me to live in your time with no servants, no luxuries, and without the love of my family? One day I want to marry a Moorish prince. I don't belong here."

"What are you planning to do?" Esther asked her.

"I need to travel into the past again in order to save my family. Would you like to come with me?"

"Your emerald will allow us to travel in time only once. If we went with you, we wouldn't be able to come back," Paul argued logically. He didn't like the idea of traveling into the past. When he and Esther dove into Cornelia's cauldron to enter Lady Rosabel's past dimension, their experience had been very difficult, even though they had the help of a witch. Additionally, going into the past meant that he had to deny the reality of his world and challenge the notion of time, which made him uncomfortable. How could his present time coexist with another time? It made no sense at all. Marrying Esther had forced him to make some mental adjustments, but Esther lived in his world and shared his life. She was real and he didn't care if she had grooved skin, pointed ears, and some innate abilities that humans don't have. Going into the past required a major conceptual revolution for him.

"No, we really can't travel with you into the past," he said, unable to sort out his unsettling thoughts.

"You'd be treated like royal guests and you'd be able to see this palace as it used to be 500 years ago," Malika enticed him.

"I'd love to see the ancient royal palace!" said Esther.

"How do we come back to the present?" Paul asked challengingly. As he was formulating this question, Malika rubbed the emerald, at the same time touching Paul and

Esther with her elbows and transferring the gem's power to them. A few seconds later, Paul, Esther, and Malika were exactly in the same spot, but in a different time frame. The Moorish building looked splendid in its original time period. Paul was awed by the gold that covered the arches. Esther admired the garden, which looked like a glorious park, filled with palm trees and exotic flowers. A carriage with six horses was parked in the path that surrounded the building. However, their surprise was quickly replaced by the anguishing realization that they had left their dimension.

"I had not really agreed to traveling in time," said Paul.

"How could you do this to us?" Esther asked the princess with indignation.

"I'm sure that my grandmother will help you return to the future. She has magic powers," said Malika.

"How exactly did you and your grandmother manage to survive when the rest of your family was poisoned?" asked Paul.

"She was in her tower waiting for a servant to bring her meal. She rarely goes to the dining room. I was asleep in my room while the servants and my family were having dinner. They ate poisoned food and died. My personal maid, who was supposed to bring my meal into my room, woke me up. *The food…it's poisoned…*, she said and collapsed next to my bed. I rubbed the topaz on my ring, becoming invisible. In the dining room, I found a ghastly scene. Ahmed was laughing for the successful outcome of his plan, holding an empty vial of poison in his hand. I rubbed the emerald, going back to a time that preceded the dinner. Ahmed caught me in his room looking for his vial of poison. As I told you, he locked me in a tower. I rubbed the emerald a second time and traveled to your time. Now that we are back in my time, we must find a way to stop Ahmed and save my family."

"Didn't you say that your grandmother has magic powers? She surely can do something. You don't need our help," Paul objected.

"Ahmed can overpower my grandmother. Although she can perform spells, she is very old and weak. I am only 16 and I need your help."

A servant interrupted their conversation. He was wearing a red turban with gold stripes, a short tunic and balloon pants. Esther thought that Dalbert would have liked his headdress. Paul found his clothes slightly unreal, as if they belonged in a fairy tale. The man was carrying a tray.

"Where would you like me to serve your tea, Princess Malika?"

"In my grandmother's tower. I'm taking two guests to her room." The servant eyed Paul and Esther with uneasiness. They were wearing modern time clothes that he had never seen before. The servant bowed and left.

"Let's talk to your grandmother," Esther proposed, understanding the gravity of the situation.

They entered the palace, which was lavishly decorated. The floors were made with different types of marble. Spectacular columns were connected by arches, adorned with elaborate arabesques. The walls were entirely painted with frescoes. The staircase that led to the room of Rashida, Malika's grandmother, was covered with elegant rugs. Malika knocked at the door and a powerful voice replied.

"Come in!"

They found the old lady sitting on a large satin pillow. Other pillows surrounded a low coffee table. Like Malika, Rashida was entirely wrapped in veils, revealing only her eyes to the guests. Her eyes seemed very sharp and had the typical metallic sparkle that Paul had learned to recognize in a witch's gaze. Malika and her two friends sat on the pillows, next to Rashida.

"Grandma, we're in trouble." She recounted her horrid discovery in the dining room and explained how she had traveled in time trying to stop Ahmed's plan.

"I'm glad you have been using the ring I gave you. Ahmed is very evil. I knew he was going to do something destructive and I was counting on you to help our family."

"With all respect, Lady Rashida, couldn't you have taken action with your magic powers?" Paul asked.

"That's precisely what I'm doing. My mission involves Malika's time travel in order to allow her to make decisions, become experienced in matters of good and evil, and be a clever sultan's wife in the future. Every kingdom is threatened by intriguing men who try to replace the rightful rulers. Ahmed is not immune to the lure of power. He wants to take control of the sultan's kingdom. I'm over 700 years old. I'm a witch, as you know, but I am physically too old to confront Ahmed alone."

"Grandma, tell us what we should do! We'll follow your instructions."

"The best way to prevent the poisoning is to make Ahmed disappear before tonight's dinner," said Rashida.

"Make him disappear? How?" Esther asked.

"We'll turn Ahmed into a fish and leave him in the royal fountain. This spell requires that you pick a ripe olive from the oldest olive tree, behind the palace. The tree is on a tall hill and I'm too old to climb and walk that far," said Rashida.

"We'll have to hurry. It's afternoon and dinner will be served a couple of hours after sunset," said Malika.

"Just a minute, Malika! While Paul and Esther pick the olive, I need you to find the largest pumpkin in our orchard. Then we'll meet in my tower and I'll cast the spell," said Rashida.

Paul and Esther parted from Malika and her grandmother. Behind the palace, they only saw one tall hill. They began to climb with a suffocating feeling of dry heat. The ground was rocky and unstable and they felt their feet slipping numerous times. The hill became very steep. They grasped low tree branches in order to continue their climb. Esther looked back and shivered. The Moorish building seemed to have lost its attractiveness. Its towers reflected an ominous shadow in the valley surrounding it.

"I'm so scared," she said.

"No, you're my brave little elf," Paul reassured her, smiling. She regained her confidence and continued to go up the slope.

"How do we know which is the oldest olive tree?" she asked.

"I have no idea. We'll take a guess," he said.

They reached the top of the hill and saw olive trees in all directions. All the trees looked alike. They walked through this olive forest until they sighted a different tree. Its trunk was a wide conglomerate of multiple tree trunks, twisted together. A motionless crow was perched on one of its branches, which carried plump, ripe olives.

"It must be this one. The bark must have taken years to grow so wide," said Paul. He picked one of the olives.

"That was easy," said Esther. As they were walking back to the palace, the crow was following them, flying very low, above their head. Esther lost her footing and began to roll down the hill. Paul ran downhill to help her, also slipping, and crashing on top of her. They helped each other up. Paul only had some cuts and scratches. Esther had a swollen ankle.

"I can't walk. I'll wait here. Take the olive to Rashida," she said.

"I lost the olive! I have to pick another one!" He climbed back to the old twisted tree. This time he picked multiple olives, in order to have extra ones. He stuffed them in his socks, inside his shirt, and in his pockets. Finally, he caught up with Esther.

"Leave me here! It's getting late!" she said.

"This place isn't safe," he said pointing at the crow that was still flying low, above their heads. He took her in his arms and carried her very slowly downhill. Malika was waiting for them near the fountain.

"What happened to Esther?" she asked. They told her about the accident and pointed at the crow that was still flying in circles above them. Malika rubbed the sapphire, at the same time touching Esther's foot, which healed instantly.

"That's amazing! Thank you," said Esther, taking a few steps.

"My goodness!" Paul remarked, noticing the enormous pumpkin inside a wheelbarrow that Malika had parked near the fountain.

"It weighs a ton! I never thought I was going to be able to lift it and put it in the wheelbarrow, but somehow it suddenly turned light," said Malika.

"Maybe it's hollow," Paul suggested. Esther tried to lift it unsuccessfully.

"It's extremely heavy!" she said.

"Did you find the right olive tree?" Malika asked them.

"I think so. I picked a lot of olives to have extra ones," said Paul. Like a magician pulling a rabbit out of his sleeve, he extracted olives out of his socks, out of his pockets, and out of the sides of his shirt, while Malika and Esther were laughing. He placed them inside the wheelbarrow, next to the pumpkin.

"How do we take the pumpkin and the olives to Rashida's tower now that the pumpkin seems to be extremely heavy?" asked Paul, who always seemed to worry about the practicality of accomplishing tasks. The three of them stared at Rashida's high tower, feeling completely at a loss. All of a sudden, an object came out of the tower window. As the object descended, they were able to see that it was a large basket attached to a rope. When the basket touched the ground, they saw a note inside that said: *Load everything!*

"How is your grandmother able to pull up the filled basket?" asked Paul.

"Magic!"

With great effort, they lifted the heavy pumpkin out of the wheelbarrow and placed it in the basket. Then, they added the olives. As they were still panting due to their physical exertion, they watched the basket float upwards at a very good speed, effortlessly. The crow kept a distance from the basket, as if it were afraid of it. After the basket disappeared inside the window, Paul and Esther continued to stare in disbelief.

"Let's go to Grandma's room! The sun will be setting soon," Malika said with urgency.

She knocked on Rashida's door.

"Come in!" said the old lady.

Paul and Esther told Rashida about the accident caused by the crow. Rashida's expression became very serious.

"The crow is a projection of Ahmed's evil soul," she explained.

"Is Ahmed a sorcerer, grandma?"

"No, he's a common, but very evil man. It's time to start the enchantment. Cut the top off and empty the pumpkin!" Paul checked inside his pockets and found the magic Swiss army knife, given to him by Haralda. He always carried it everywhere. However, he was surprised that the knife had traveled in time inside his pocket. When the pumpkin was ready, Rashida took one of the olives and placed it inside the pumpkin.

"The pumpkin is a magic kiln of transformation. The olive will give us its precious oil. Since you picked many olives, Paul, we might as well use them all," she said. Rashida placed her hands over the filled pumpkin and looked at the red sky, outside her window. Paul and Esther had the impression that the pumpkin had turned into an incandescent red bowl. The veil covering Rashida's head began to shake and suddenly flew off, revealing the witch's face. Her features were terrifying. She produced a high-pitched scream. Outside, the crow knocked on the window with its beak. The sun disappeared behind the hills. A soft darkness replaced the bright redness of the sky. The crow was barely visible behind the window. Rashida's veil was wrapped around her head again. The pumpkin had reacquired its normal orange coloring. Malika lit the lanterns in the room.

"You can look inside the pumpkin now," said the witch. They looked and gasped. The pumpkin was filled with a golden liquid.

"Magic oil," said the witch with satisfaction.

"What do we do next?" Paul asked.

"Malika will call Ahmed to my room so that we can anoint him before dinner is served," she replied with a cackle.

As soon as Malika left, Rashida gave instructions to Paul.

"You must pour the contents of this pumpkin on Ahmed's head when he's in my room."

Malika returned with the Grand Vizier.

"Did you summon me?" the Grand Vizier asked Rashida.

"Yes, Ahmed. I'd like you to look out of my window and tell me if you can see anything unusual." Ahmed stared at the sky, without understanding. The crow knocked at the window with its beak, startling him.

"Do you recognize that crow?" Rashida asked him.

Ahmed shivered, without understanding.

"That crow has the color of your soul," she told him. He seemed paralyzed with fear. Behind him, Paul lifted the large pumpkin, which contrary to his expectations, seemed to be very light. He poured the oil on Ahmed's head. Instantly, the Grand Vizier turned into a carp with red and gold stripes. Paul and Esther stared in amazement.

"In the fountain!" said Rashida. Paul, Esther, and Malika walked to the fountain and released the carp. The crow began to fly in circles, above the fountain. All of a sudden, it dive-bombed and attacked Malika. She screamed and immediately rubbed the ruby on her ring. The crow's beak went through her body, without hurting her. After multiple attempts, the crow flew away. Malika tried to sit on the side of the fountain, next to her friends, who had been watching the crow's attacks with horror. However, her body was immaterial and she couldn't sit on the fountain.

"It's my body! It's visible, but I have to get it back!" she said, while Paul and Esther continued to stare at her, petrified with panic. She rubbed the ruby and was finally able to sit. Malika and her friends enjoyed the crisp sound of the falling water, quietly recovering from their frightful experience.

"Now that we succeeded in preventing the poisoning of the food, let's have a dinner celebration!" said Malika. They got up from the fountain and walked towards the palace. Paul felt relieved when he saw that Malika was leaving footprints on the path.

At the dinner table, Paul and Esther sat between Rashida and Malika. They enjoyed a sumptuous meal that included exotic skewers, shrimps with peppers and rice, meats seasoned with Middle Eastern spices, and Moorish paella. One of the servants entered the dining hall, holding a large plate. He announced that he had found a large carp with red and gold stripes and had especially cooked it for the royal dinner. Paul and Esther turned to Rashida with a concerned expression on their face.

"Relax! The carp was an instrument of my magic, but it's just a carp. After the transformation, Ahmed turned into the crow that initially was only a projection of his evil soul," Rashida explained with a smile. Paul stared at the carp with suspicion. It had a delicious smell. He gave up on understanding magic and filled his plate.

"If Ahmed has turned into the crow, I understand why the crow attacked me," said Malika.

"Where is the crow now?" asked Esther.

"It died when the cook roasted the carp. I'm very grateful to you and Paul for helping us defeat the evil man that could have destroyed our family. I have a gift for you.

When you are ready to travel to your time, rub this gem holding your husband's hand," said Rashida. She gave an emerald ring to Esther, who thanked the good witch.

After the dinner party, Paul, Esther, and Malika went to the fountain one last time. It was a beautiful starry night. They sat on the side of the fountain and chatted for a while.

"Are you ready to go back to your time?" Malika asked.

"We are," said Esther.

"Who knows: maybe we'll meet again one day!" said Paul. They hugged Malika and said goodbye. Esther held her husband's hand and rubbed the emerald. A few seconds later, Malika was no longer sitting with them on the fountain.

"This building still looks fabulous today," said Esther. She and Paul enjoyed the gentle sound of the cascading water.

"Would you like to visit the city of Granada?" Paul asked her. She paused for a few moments.

"I'd rather leave Spain and go straight to the creek to retrieve Jarman's chest," she replied.

"Good idea! I'd like to go home and find out what's happening in the village and in Green Wood," said Paul. Unknowingly, the couple had a feeling that something terrible was going to happen and felt compelled to return home.

"It's time to use our last wish. I'd like to go back to the creek," said Esther, holding Paul's hand.

7

The Crystal Water Lily

Paul and Esther were standing again on the path near the creek. They felt happy to be back in their familiar environment.

"There is a shovel next to the oak tree," Esther pointed out.

"Whoever controls these gems thinks of everything," Paul exclaimed. He dug out the antique chest.

"I hope Jarman will let me buy this chest," he added, admiring its wood carving. As they started walking in the direction of Jarman's house, they heard someone whistling a lively Irish tune, accompanied by the sound of a magic fiddle, in the distance.

"Would you like to stop for a dance?" Paul asked. Esther gave him an ecstatic smile. They engaged in a very fast Irish jig, hopping and spinning merrily in the wood.

"Good afternoon!" Jarman greeted them, interrupting his whistled tune, while the fiddle music ceased.

"Oh, it's you! Thank you for the good music!" said Esther.

"Hello, Jarman! I see that you're going fishing," said Paul, noticing that the old elf was holding a bucket and a fishing rod.

"Yes. I'm going to catch trout for dinner. Are you still on your honeymoon?"

"We are. This honeymoon is taking us to unforeseen places," Esther replied.

"We just came back from a complicated mission that involved time traveling to 16th century Spain," said Paul.

"It's good to be back in our wood. We were heading in the direction of your house. We'd like to give you the green diamonds that we found in Osmar's fountain. I know they belong to you," said Esther, handing the chest to him. Jarman's eyes lit up because he had a true passion for his gem collection. He put down his fishing gear and took the chest carefully in his hands. He opened it and stared at the green diamonds almost in a hypnotic state.

"They are very rare and of exceptional quality," he assessed.

"They grant wishes!" Esther told him.

"I know. They are magic."

"They definitely added some thrill into our life," Paul said with a tone that didn't sound very positive. Like a little boy holding his favorite marbles, Jarman tightened his grip around the gems and placed them in his pocket.

"You can keep the chest. It's not magic, but I'm sure it will be useful to you," he told Paul, who felt like he had just won the lottery.

"Did anything remarkable happen in the village or in Green Wood, while we were gone?" asked Esther.

"Well…ahem…yes…You don't know yet?"

"Know what? We just returned from 16th century Grenada," said Paul.

"You should go home then. I don't want to spoil your surprise," said Jarman, picking up his fishing gear. He resumed his whistling and quickly walked downstream.

Paul and Esther rushed into the village and went to Paul's house. Rebecca was very happy to see both of them. She had formed a genuine bond of friendship with her sister-in-law and no longer cared that she was an elf. Esther was her brother's wife and part of the family. She hugged them, bombarding them with questions.

"Where have you been? I was worried about you. Are you feeling alright?

Were you involved in another magic adventure?"

"We're fine. We've been enjoying ourselves traveling," Paul answered, omitting to specify the type of travel since he knew that Rebecca worried too much.

"What's on your finger?" asked Esther, with the unfailing acumen of her womanly nature. Rebecca extended her hand showcasing a large diamond ring and started crying. At the same time, she tried to explain her predicament.

"David and I got engaged. We're getting married next week. I was so worried that you wouldn't come back on time," she said, continuing to cry desperately.

"Is that why you're crying?" said Paul, trying to comfort her with another hug.

"No, I'm crying for another reason."

"Aren't you happy to marry David?" Esther asked.

"Yes, I love David. I'm crying for another reason...Something terrible happened this morning...A horrible old woman came to visit... It was terrifying!" she said, while sobbing convulsively.

"For heaven's sake, what happened Rebecca?" Paul started to lose his patience.

"Why don't we all sit down and you tell us what happened from the beginning," Esther suggested in an accommodating manner. Paul and Esther grabbed Rebecca's arms and led her to the living room couch. Then, they sat in front of Rebecca, patiently waiting for her to calm down.

"I was eating breakfast when I heard a loud knock on the door. I thought it was you. I rushed to open the door, but instead I saw an old woman holding a cat in her arms. Both the woman and the cat were looking at me with a mean expression. *Do you recognize my cat?* the woman asked me. The cat did look familiar, but I wasn't sure. *Not really*, I said, making her very angry."

"What did the cat look like?" Esther interrupted.

"It was a large cat, with long hair, red and black stripes, and yellow eyes."

"That's the same cat that snatched me and then chased me when we were going to Rylan's castle," said Esther. Paul turned very serious and concerned. Rebecca resumed her narration.

"*You don't remember my cat?* she asked me. *I must have seen him before, but I don't remember where*, I said. *This is Gorman!* she yelled, making the house shake. *Your silly cat beat Gorman at the AACC this year!*"

"What's the AACC?" asked Esther.

"The Annual All Cat Competition that is held in our village. It attracts cat owners from all over Ireland. All pedigree and non-purebred cats are allowed to compete. A panel of judges selects the winner based on appearance, gait, fur condition, and other physical criteria. It's a big affair that lasts three days because a large number of non-pure cats are entered in the contest," Rebecca explained.

"And your cat won first place?" Esther asked in astonishment.

"Yes, Bo won first place and apparently Gorman came in second." As he heard his name, Rebecca's cat slowly made an entrance in the living room. He was truly a gorgeous, large, black cat, with dark orange and white spots, and green eyes. Rebecca picked him up and held him in her arms as she continued her narration.

"*I used a little magic to improve Gorman's appearance and, yet, your silly cat managed to win!*" said the old woman."

Paul and Esther gasped realizing that Rebecca's visitor was an angry witch.

"*I'm very unhappy!* she screamed. *Gorman is like a dear child to me. I've had him for many years. He deserved to win first place at the AACC. You will pay for this!* she yelled, making the house shake again. *I know that you're getting married next week. What a special day in your life! However, all your children will never know happiness nor success!* she shouted and then disappeared. I haven't told David about the incident because I don't want to worry him," said Rebecca, crying desperately.

"Who owns Gorman?" asked Paul

"I don't know. I can't even remember that her cat was in the competition. So many people participate in the AACC. Do you really think she is a witch?" Rebecca asked, lowering her voice almost to a whisper.

"Yes, she is a witch! She cursed your children and she vanished!" her brother answered.

"Goodness gracious! I never thought I would be stuck in a situation that involves a witch! I don't go looking for trouble like you do!" said Rebecca.

"Let's pay a visit to Lodema the witch. She will know who owns Gorman," said Esther, interrupting a conversation that was slowly escalating to an argument.

"Please hurry! I'm afraid that David won't marry me anymore..." said Rebecca sobbing.

Paul and Esther rushed to Lodema's house, while discussing the serious problem.

"Both Rebecca and Bo are in danger. That curse is probably only part of the witch's revenge plan," said Esther.

"It's never good to make a witch angry. She could turn Rebecca into a lizard and let Gorman have her," said Paul, shaking his head.

"She could do a lot worse than that!" said Esther. In reality, neither one of them had fully comprehended the extent of the possible implications of the matter. They reached Lodema's unusual cottage, which was on top of a hill, on an isolated side of the wood. Her dog, Rufus, ran down the hill, wagging his tail to greet them. He had been bred from a golden retriever and a black Labrador and looked like a sweet golden retriever with black fur. Paul and Esther petted him and followed him uphill. Lodema's cottage was a culinary spectacle. Its roof was made with fudge-swirled chocolate brownies. The drainpipes consisted of long cannoli filled with sweet ricotta cheese. No one knew how the rainwater was actually carried to the ground. The chimney was made of shortbread cookies. The walls were layers of white cake, vanilla custard mixed with whipped cream, and raspberry jam. The shutters were chocolate bars. Cookies with red, purple, and green icing were attached to the wall as decorative tiles. The front door knob was a blueberry cupcake. A fountain with colorful jets of pink and yellow lemonade stood in the front yard. Paul and Esther hesitated before knocking and instead pulled off the cupcake and other baked goods, filling their stomach. As soon as a piece of the house was pulled off, a new one magically replaced it. They also gave a few cookies to Rufus, who was barking insistently to have his share. Then, they drank from the fountain. Finally, they knocked at the door and a pleasant looking, middle-aged woman opened the door. Lodema had violet eyes, which sparkled like bright amethysts. Paul felt slightly dazzled by her gaze.

"Come in!" She led them into an enclosed veranda overlooking the backyard.

"Please, don't mind my husband, Jack. He's pruning some bushes in the garden." Lodema the witch and Captain Jack Sanders had met on a cruise ship, touring the Mediterranean. They both loved to travel and every summer they left the Irish wood to visit a new place. Captain Sanders lived happily in Green Wood, without regrets, but during the summer he enjoyed reattaching a few ties with the human community, while his wife disguised her witch identity and her magic powers. Like all wise witches, Lodema never revealed herself to strangers. Paul and Esther sat on a couch, surrounded by daffodils, marigolds, and periwinkles.

"Jack loves gardening and makes our house look fabulous. What is the reason for your visit?" asked Lodema, stopping Paul's mental images of daffodils and cupcakes.

"We would like to know who owns Gorman, the big red and black cat that took second place at the AACC this year," Paul replied.

"Gorman belongs to Renalda the witch. He's as mean as she is. Did something happen?" asked Lodema.

"As a matter of fact, Renalda cursed my sister Rebecca's future children because Rebecca's cat won first place at the cat competition. My sister is supposed to get married next week," Paul explained with a strained voice. Lodema seemed stunned and kept quiet for a while. The clicking of Captain

Sanders' shears could be clearly heard through the glass window.

"This is a very serious problem. It's difficult because Renalda is very powerful and I don't believe for a second that her revenge could be that simple," she said. Lodema remained thoughtful and finally seemed to have decided on a course of action.

"We'll take the dearest thing to her, meaning Gorman, and then ask her to remove the curse as ransom," Lodema proposed. Paul and Esther didn't show any enthusiasm for this plan, which seemed risky and full of loose ends. However, they knew that Lodema was an experienced witch, capable of tackling magic problems.

"It's a long shot…How do we kidnap Gorman?" asked Paul.

"That cat is always wandering around the woods, chasing his victims. He could be anywhere," said Esther.

"Rufus can certainly find Gorman! He has an excellent sense of smell," said Lodema. She opened a cabinet and took out a folded mesh fabric.

"Follow Rufus and when he locates the cat, throw this special net on Gorman, pull the string, and trap him inside the sack! This net can magically adjust to the size of the prey. It will look wide when you throw it on Gorman, but then it will shrink turning into a pouch when you pull the string.

Gorman won't be able to escape. Take him to my house!" said Lodema. She called Rufus, looked into his eyes and said:

"Find Gorman!" Then she walked her visitors with Rufus to the front door and waved goodbye. Rufus was devoted to Lodema. He would have done anything for her and even risked his life to save her, if necessary. However, he was afraid of Gorman, who looked more like a tiger than a cat. Rufus unwillingly embarked on this search, followed by Paul and Esther. As they walked through the trees, Rufus could detect Gorman's scent everywhere because the cat liked to chase small animals throughout the woods. Rufus knew he wasn't on the right track. He slowed down his pace, unable to decide on a specific direction. He was heartbroken because he didn't want to disappoint Lodema, but he had no idea of where to find Gorman.

"We'll be walking all day without tracking down the cat, if we keep following this clueless dog," Paul said suddenly.

"There is a way to find Gorman, although I don't like it," said Esther. Paul looked at her with expectation, particularly since Rufus had stopped to smell a patch of flowers.

"We could go where Gorman grabbed me, on the way to Rylan's house. Gorman probably likes to hang out in that area. Hopefully I'll catch his attention and he'll go after me again," Esther proposed.

"In other words, you'll be a decoy. It's dangerous, but it may work. We don't really have other choices," Paul said, noticing that Rufus was now running around playfully, with a large twig in his mouth. They called Rufus and started walking in the direction of Rylan's house, while Lodema's dog was now following them. Since Rylan the goblin had lost all his magic powers, they knew that they would not shrink while approaching his house. Suddenly, Rufus started barking insistently.

"Gorman must be around here," said Paul. Like a lightning bolt, the cat pounced from behind a tree, grabbed Esther with his teeth, and ran away. Both Paul and Rufus chased him while Esther was screaming. Gorman kept going in and out of sight as he ran through the bushes and among the trees. However, Esther's screams allowed them to continue in the right direction. Esther managed to kick Gorman on his nose. The cat growled in pain, opening his mouth. Esther slipped out of his jaws and started running towards Paul and Rufus. Gorman chased after her, approaching Paul, who covered him with the magic net and pulled the string trapping him. Barking with satisfaction, Rufus started running in circles around the captured cat, who was meowing loudly inside the sack. Paul and Esther stopped for a few minutes to catch their breath and walked back to Lodema's house. Rufus kept his eyes on the mesh sack the entire time and Gorman stared at Rufus with contempt. As soon as she opened the door, Lodema hugged Rufus, stroking him warmly behind his ears, while he responded affectionately with soft grunts.

"You're such a wonderful dog! I knew you could find him!" she told Rufus. Paul and Esther looked at each other in astonishment, but let Rufus take all the credit.

"What are we going to do with Gorman?" asked Esther. The cat growled inside the sack.

"Gorman will stay in my house while we send a ransom note to Renalda." Lodema wrote a message on a sheet of paper. Then, she folded it and addressed Rufus.

"Go to Renalda's house and bring this note to her!" As he heard the name of the evil witch, Rufus lowered his ears, licked his lips several times, and gave a whine.

"No need to complain! Renalda will be happy when she receives my message," Lodema told him with a soothing voice. Although he was totally not convinced, like Paul and Esther, Rufus took the paper in his mouth and left, followed by Paul and Esther. While walking to Renalda's house, he saw squirrels and lizards running among the trees and regained his high spirits. He was tempted to chase them, but he was a very reliable dog. He continued his walk, planning to have some fun on the way back.

Renalda's house was located in a remote and fairly inaccessible area, facing a ravine. It was surrounded by thorny bushes, tall trees, and nettles. It looked like a shack with barred windows, broken shutters, weeds and vines covering most of the walls. A thick, black smoke rose from the chimney. Paul and Esther hid behind a bush, while Rufus walked to the front door and barked several times. The door made a loud squeaking sound as it slowly opened. The tall, imposing figure of Renalda the witch came into view. Her green eyes reflected a variety of shades of soft sage, sharp pine, and dry moss. Her long black hair spiraled into intricate coils constantly in motion, like snakes ready to constrict their prey.

"What brings you to this side of the wood?" she asked with a sweet voice. Rufus felt confused by the mesmerizing effect of her voice and the glittering light in her eyes.

"You have a message for me! Let me have it!" she said, when she saw the paper in his mouth. Her order had the sudden effect of a crashing wave. Rufus released the ransom note. Renalda read it and emitted a loud scream that reverberated through the woods.

"*...reverse the curse on Rebecca's future children immediately or something terrible will happen to Gorman!*" she read a second time and burst into an explosive laughter that shook the walls and windows of her house. One of the shutters fell off the wall. Renalda turned into a ball of fire and swirled, producing ribbons of smoke. Her hair curls were glowing flames out of control. Rufus flattened his body on the ground, hiding his tail under his belly. Paul and Esther watched, petrified with fear. Renalda stopped circling and regained her human form. She stood very tall, taller than her house and taller than the trees, or that's how Rufus perceived her from his flattened position.

"Give my answer to Lodema!" she told Rufus after writing a message on the reverse side of the ransom note. She also handed him a biscuit, which he politely took in his mouth. However, as soon as he was out of Renalda's sight, he cleverly spit it out. He had lived in the witches' world long enough not to trust Renalda. He crossed the wood a second time and, to his chagrin, he had to ignore the squirrels, the lizards, and the field mice he wished to chase and play with. His duty and loyalty to Lodema came first. Rufus, Paul, and Esther reached Lodema's cottage. Lodema received Rufus with praises and cupcakes, which he devoured happily. Then, she unfolded the paper and read loudly:

"You have 12 hours to give me Gorman or I will burn the wood!"

Everyone gasped horrified.

"Can she really burn the entire wood?" asked Esther.

"Yes, she can turn into a ball of fire and roll through the wood, destroying as she pleases," Lodema replied with serious concern.

"However, you could stop the fire instantly! You are a witch!" Paul exclaimed.

"I can stop a natural fire in an instant, but I cannot neutralize Renalda's flames. When she turns into a ball of fire, she's not casting a spell. Fire is part of her," Lodema explained.

"The only way to stop her is to act upon her identity," Esther rationalized.

"Yes, but I don't know how we can impact such a strong witch," said Lodema.

"Possibly Jarman may have an answer," Esther suggested.

"He's experienced with magic gems and he's very old. He may know some magic stone that could neutralize Renalda's power," said Lodema.

"We'll go straight to his house. He should be back from fishing," said Paul.

When they reached Jarman's treehouse, Paul banged the hammer on the large pan hanging from a low branch, producing a loud gong.

"I'll be right there!" Jarman announced from a high branch of a distant tree. Like an agile Tarzan, he swung from tree to tree, using his system of ropes, he crossed a little bridge connecting a high branch to a lower level, and finally came down to the entrance on a rope ladder.

"Your house is really a lot of fun!" commented Paul.

"I never stopped having fun since I was a young elf," he chuckled, satisfied.

"We come from Lodema's house. We're in an emergency situation," said Esther.

"What happened?" the old elf asked in alarm.

"Renalda the witch cursed Rebecca's future children. Lodema kidnapped her cat Gorman, and asked for the reversal of the curse as ransom. However, Renalda replied that we have 12 hours to give her Gorman, or she'll burn the wood," Esther told him in one breath. Jarman became very angry when he heard that Renalda was threatening to burn the wood.

"I won't let that witch destroy my treehouse!" he blasted.

"We could release Gorman, but that won't solve Rebecca's problem, and Lodema thinks that Renalda's revenge plan may not be complete," said Esther.

"Lodema said that we need an object that may affect Renalda's ability to turn into a ball of fire because fire is part of her identity," said Paul.

Jarman sighed a few times and finally offered his counsel like an oracle.

"You need the crystal water lily."

"What is it?" Paul and Esther asked simultaneously.

"It's a large water lily made of pink tourmaline. It's in the Quartz Cave, behind the high waterfall. Taking it won't be easy because it's guarded by Aldor's spirit. Aldor is a sorcerer who lived over 500 years ago. He was more powerful than any witch and his spirit has retained all the powers he had when he was alive," Jarman told them.

"Behind the waterfall? How do we enter this cave?" asked Paul, disregarding the description of the water lily and of the sorcerer, as he thought that the Quartz Cave was impossible to access.

"I'll go with you and help you," said Jarman, who was determined to save the wood.

They walked along the creek downstream for a few hours. Gradually, the creek grew in size and turned into a river. The speed of the water flow increased and turbulent rapids became visible throughout the river. The path sharply dropped to a lower level. As they followed the new lower path, they finally saw the waterfall. It had a very high drop that formed a white vortex. With difficulty, walking on slippery rocks, they followed a narrow ledge along the wall of the cliff, reaching the area behind the waterfall. The entrance into the cave was dark and damp. Jarman took a match out of his pocket and pronounced the following magic words: *"Give me a bright flame and stay the same!"* The match lit up instantly. The flame produced a bright light, without burning down the match. Inside the cave, the quartz was dark and smoky in some areas, and light pink in others. On the ground, surrounded by sparkling amethyst quartz, the large crystal water lily radiated a white light.

"Is it radioactive?" asked Paul.

"No, just magic," Jarman replied.

"It's completely embedded in amethyst quartz. We have to extract it. I guess my magic Swiss army knife will be able to cut through the rock," said Paul.

"Don't touch my water lily!" a booming voice resounded inside the cave.

They looked around and couldn't see anyone.

"Who are you?" asked Esther.

"Aldor. If you touch my water lily, you'll die instantly."

"Where are you?" asked Paul, who couldn't understand where the voice was coming from.

"I'm in the water lily. Before you touch my crystal, you have to prove to be worthy of it. The crystal water lily is not for everybody."

"What shall we do?" asked Paul.

"You must dive into the waterfall. If you survive the vortex, you'll find the water lily on the riverbank." Paul and Esther shivered at the thought of diving into the vortex. They walked out of the cave and lined up behind the waterfall.

"Are you ready to jump?" asked Jarman. His voice was muffled by the deafening sound of the crashing waterfall. They looked at the vortex at the bottom of the precipice. Esther shook her head negatively.

"I can swim, but I doubt I can reemerge from that strong whirlpool," Paul replied.

"Don't worry, I don't know how to swim either, but I may have something that can help us," said Jarman.

"I wish we still had the temporary gills that Cornelia had given to us," said Esther. Jarman searched one of his pockets and took out three small pieces of dry kelp. He gave one to Paul and Esther and kept one for himself.

"After we eat this magic kelp, we won't need to breathe underwater," said Jarman.

"Where did you get this kelp?" asked Paul.

"It was a gift. A couple of hundred years ago, a sorcerer friend of mine needed some special rocks. I was able to find them for him and he paid me back with these pieces of magic kelp. I never thought I was going to need them," said Jarman.

"Business gifts always come in handy," Paul acknowledged. They chewed the kelp and swallowed it. Esther was first in line, but she was hesitant to jump. She was shivering like a wet kitten.

"Renalda will burn our wood! We must jump in and hurry!" said Jarman.

"I really don't think I can do it," said Esther, mortified.

"In that case, I will jump holding you in my arms," said Paul. He lifted Esther into his arms, closed his eyes, and leaped. They had the impression that a very long time elapsed before they touched the bottom of the waterfall, although it took only a few seconds. Once submerged, they were pulled to the bottom of the river in a spiral movement. Paul released Esther and each one of them began to swim underwater, following the flow of the river. Then, they tried to resurface, but the currents continued to pull them underwater. When the river speed finally slowed down, they were able to reach the surface and swim to one of the banks. Paul came out first and helped Esther. Jarman seemed to be extremely fit, in spite of his old age.

"That was quite a jolly experience!" said the old elf, feeling completely exhilarated, as he came out of the river. Paul and Esther stared at him, while trying to regain their body heat in the sun.

"My goodness!" was Esther's understated reaction when she saw the crystal water lily gloriously shining in the sunlight. The flower was about 10 inches in diameter. Its petals had various shades of a red-rose color.

"Spectacular!" Jarman remarked, while his eyes sparkled with joy.

"Are we allowed to touch it now?" asked Paul. A tall, dark figure appeared on the riverbank, smiling.

"You're brave! I'll let you borrow my water lily because I know you need it for a good cause. However, you must return it to me when you complete your mission. Good luck!" said Aldor before disappearing.

"What do we do with this flower?" asked Esther, timidly touching its petals.

"The crystal will strike Renalda's identity when she turns into a ball of fire. This magic rock has a strong cooling power," explained Jarman. They walked back upstream, and, several hours later, they reached the area where the river narrowed to the size of a creek. Lodema was waiting for them. She saw the crystal water lily in Jarman's arms.

"Excellent! 12 hours have almost elapsed. I'm sure that Renalda will show up soon." Suddenly, a loud explosion shook the ground like an earthquake. A spiraling ball of fire appeared, while a piercing scream traveled through the wood.

"Where is Gorman?" asked Renalda, whose face had become visible among the flames. Her mouth was twisted in a ferocious expression, revealing her long, sharp witch's teeth. Her eyes reflected her mad rage.

"I'm not giving you Gorman," said Lodema, holding the crystal water lily. As the crystal reflected its light on her face, Lodema clearly enunciated:

"The wood will be alive forever, as in a fairy tale. The trees will stand together. My plan won't fail."

"Is that some sort of spell?" Renalda asked, laughing. "Are you holding a magic ingredient?" she said, mocking Lodema. "Where's Gorman?" she thundered.

"You'll never know," Lodema replied. The infuriated witch transformed into a fast-spinning ball of flames and began to roll among the trees, lighting them on fire. Quickly, Lodema threw the crystal water lily on top of Renalda, causing a burst of sparks. The water lily turned dark red and seemed to also be on fire. Paul and Esther weren't sure if they should have watched or closed their eyes to avoid witnessing the impending destruction of the wood. Lodema stretched her arms out, while waves of energy traveled from the tip of her fingers towards the trees, shaking them from the base to the top. The entire wood seemed to be possessed by a mysterious force that made all branches sway together. Lodema invoked the power of the South winds. Immediately, jets of warm air blew through the wood, accelerating the spreading of the fire, as Renalda's ball of flames continued to roll from tree to tree. Jarman, Paul, and Esther watched with horror. Lodema was worsening the situation. Just when they lost all hope, Lodema stared at the water lily, which turned into a blue flower made of ice.

"Freeze the inferno!" she said while her violet eyes shone like the blinding rays of the midday sun. Paul and Esther hugged each other terrified. Jarman had lost all his spunk and stood in front of the burning wood like a weak old man. The icy water lily radiated a blue light, which was transported by the energy waves that connected all the trees. It gradually extinguished the flames on the trees and it slowed down the spiral movement of the ball, eventually halting it, while a black ribbon of smoke slowly rose into the sky. And suddenly it was cold. An icy breeze blew through the wood. A few flakes of snow fell on all the branches and on the ground. The ball of fire had turned into an inert small piece of charcoal. Next to it, on the ground, the crystal water lily triumphantly radiated its natural pinkish coloring.

"Where is Renalda?" Esther asked, shivering.

"The crystal water lily cooled off her fiery nature. Her identity was permanently undermined and she no longer exists. Her curse on Rebecca's children won't take effect, and the wood is safe," Lodema announced, regaining the pleasant appearance of a simple, middle-aged woman. The tall, dark figure of Aldor's ghost was standing next to her.

"I'm glad that my water lily helped destroy evil and brought order back in this part of the world," he said. He picked up his water lily and vanished.

Lodema said goodbye, walked back to her cottage, and joined her husband in the garden. Unaware of the extraordinary events that were occurring in the wood, Captain Sanders had mistaken the distant explosions for hunters' gunshots. He smiled at his wife serenely.

"There is a cat trapped in a sack, in the veranda," he mentioned.

"Yes, I almost forgot. I have to change him into a good house pet. Maybe he and Rufus can become friends," said Lodema. He accepted her plan at its face value because he knew never to question a witch's words.

In the woods, the cold winds were calming down. The snow was beginning to melt.

"I'm going to check on my treehouse," said Jarman, leaving. Paul and Esther sat on a rock to rest.

"Rebecca will be happy that the curse was reversed," said Paul.

"I wonder who will attend the wedding," said Esther.

"Yes…I wonder how many guests and…*what kind* of guests will attend," said Paul.

"No matter what happens, you must promise that we will dance some Irish jigs on the field. Our honeymoon is still not over," she said with an elfish expression in her eyes.

Paul stared at her with concern. Magic had shown up at their door too many times already.

Printed by Amazon Italia Logistica S.r.l.
Torrazza Piemonte (TO), Italy